Redemption in Eden

Patricia Jones

First published 2019
Published by GB Publishing Org

Copyright © 2019 Patricia Jones
All rights reserved
ISBN: 978-1-912576-32-6 (hardback)
978-1-912576-33-3 (paperback)
978-1-912576-34-0 (eBook)
978-1-912576-35-7 (Kindle)

Cover Design © 2019 Tillier Designs
Cover Illustration by Nick Gott

GB Publishing Org
www.gbpublishing.co.uk

Dedication

Redemption in Eden is dedicated to my brother, Bill Johnson in memory of the happy, sunny afternoon when together we devised the *1937 Jackson-Johnson* classic car.

CONTENTS

REDEMPTION IN EDEN

WELCOME TO THE VILLAGE OF EDEN BRIDGE
ON THE STAFFORDSHIRE-DERBYSHIRE BORDERS

NEWCOMERS TO STONEY LEA FARMHOUSE
Tom and Kitty Munroe – in search of a rural idyll
Sasha and Midge – their children

THEIR FAMILY AND FRIENDS
Ted and Simone Munroe – Tom's parents
Chris and Melissa Munroe – Tom's older brother and sister-in-law
Dominic and Tristan Munroe – their twin sons
Viktoria Benhalmi – the current au pair

George and Betty Oxley – Kitty's parents

Roland (Rollo) Cowper-Smythe –Tom's oldest friend
Sue and Mike Pearman – Kitty's closest friends
Lottie and Luke – their children

ESTABLISHED EDEN BRIDGE INHABITANTS

MANOR FARM
Mark and Beth Willoughby – farming one of the largest farms in the county
Alice and Harry – their children

THE GOAT SHED
Izzie Buchann – single mum and arty type
Xavier – her son

REEVE HOUSE
Mrs Finchcock (Esther) – The Women's Institute (WI) matriarch and organiser of village and church events
Richard Finchcock – her kind and reliable green-fingered husband

OTHER EDEN BRIDGE RESIDENTS
Mrs Selby – a gossip who runs the local shop and post office
Mrs Dale – leader of the playgroup
Mrs Drummond – headteacher of the village school
Danny Morland – plumber and Elvis Presley fanatic
Max Fielding – the vet
Phil Hogarth – the farrier

LEAVING EDEN BRIDGE
Dora and David Redman

VISITORS TO EDEN BRIDGE
Alex Finchcock – a London based architect - a regular weekend visitor
Tivadar Czinege – a man on a mission
Joe Saxon – who has lost his way
Frannie Saxon – who finds him

ANIMALS
Spark and Billy – sensible sheepdogs
Artie – a devious fox terrier
Dilly and Dally – bottle-fed lambs
Holly and Ivy – Christmas kittens
Daisy – a lost, bedraggled creature
Kong – her son
Gilda and Drusilla – music loving goats
Molly, Polly, Henny, Penny, Clucky and Lucky – chickens
A pair of tawny owls

Redemption in Eden

The end of the Idyll

"Love divine, all loves excelling,
Joy of heaven, to earth come down;
fix in us thy humble dwelling;
all thy faithful mercies crown!"

'Wasn't that one of their wedding hymns? Such a lovely wedding. Pity it ended like this.'

Kitty Munroe, ramrod stiff under the borrowed hat, recognised the smoker's rasp of her Great Auntie Marjorie's whisper. According to family lore Great Auntie Marjorie had never discovered the meaning of tact. Kitty, mouthing the familiar words, prayed that compassion would enter her "trembling heart".

It had indeed been a lovely wedding, a golden, late summer's day in another beautiful country church. Not even her mother-in-law's tight-lipped disapproval of their choice of music had spoilt their day.

Now the same friends and family were once more gathered in another flower filled country church not to celebrate a joyful union but an untimely death.

As the last strains of the hymn died away Rollo squeezed Kitty's arm before stepping up to the lectern to deliver a tribute to his best friend and Kitty's husband.

Kitty, didn't listen to the familiar tale of how, when Rollo had first met Tom at the age of seven, they had hated each other on sight. The ridiculous exploits of school and university and some of the less salacious anecdotes of their adventures washed over her. Tom, a natural sportsman, had excelled at

3

everything and somehow had persuaded and encouraged the less agile and more academic Rollo to realise goals that anyone else of his build, stature and temperament would not have found possible.

As Rollo's calm voice explained how Tom had managed to achieve a happy balance between work and recreation and, as an enthusiastic team member he'd been an inspiration to others, Kitty concentrated on the over large flower arrangement her mother-in-law had insisted the florist place on a plinth by the chancel steps. Already the delicate peonies were beginning to droop and a few pale pink petals carpeted the black and terracotta tiles.

When Rollo began to speak of Tom's relationship with herself and their children Kitty felt tears stinging her eyes and she forced herself to recall her last visit to the dentist. She relived the sharp sting of the anaesthetic as the syringe entered her gum and the wet whoosh of the drill working away at her tooth. But her thoughts of dentists, drills and the pain they evoked just brought back memories of Tom's wide, warm smile and his special grin when she eventually agreed to anything and everything he'd suggested.

Tom had been the one who had wanted to move to the country. He'd conjured up the picture of a rural idyll; of the children, bonny and blithe playing in an apple laden orchard, with a donkey for them to ride and fresh eggs straight from their own hens for breakfast. It had been Tom who'd gone online and contacted estate agents and had finally shown her the old farmhouse on a golden autumn afternoon. If truth be told, she had needed very little persuading as she had fallen in love with the house as quickly and as easily as she had fallen in love with Tom ten years before.

The comfortable reassuring weight of her father's arm around her shoulders made her aware that Rollo was bringing his eulogy to a close on a positive and reassuring note.

'Good old Roland,' her father whispered. 'He always comes up trumps. You've got a good friend there, love.'

Kitty nodded and tightened her hold on her father's hand. During the horror of the last weeks she'd come to appreciate not just Rollo's staunch friendship but the love and loyalty of her parents and her friends.

'Dear Lord, look in mercy on Tom and all who mourn his passing.
Give them faith in times of darkness.
Let your peace strengthen them with the knowledge of your infinite love.'

4

The resonant voice of Andy, the Team Rector, brought the service to its inevitable close. The congregation rose as the wicker coffin was carried out of the church into the bright June sunshine.

Kitty had dreaded the next stage of the proceedings. On the way home she tried to put the finality of the brief ceremony at the crematorium out of her mind, preferring to concentrate on the catering arrangements. The closing of the curtains and the poignant strains of *Hallelujah* had made the reality of Tom's death absolute.

'Kitty, I need a large bowl or a dish?' Kitty turned to see her sister-in-law, tottering on her spiky heels on the kitchen's uneven flagstones, holding a large plastic container. 'I've made my special fruit salad. I thought it'll be refreshing as it's turned out so hot.' Melissa Munroe gave her a warm smile.

'The cut glass bowls are in the dining room sideboard or there's baking bowls in the kitchen dresser but ...'

'Thank you Kit, just leave it to me. I'm sure I'll find something suitable. You run along and see to your guests.'

Thus dismissed Kitty drifted back into the throng of Tom's colleagues, sporting friends, classic car enthusiasts and family and neighbours who had spread out into the garden and were chatting and gossiping just as if they were at a garden party instead of at a country wake.

Kit found a glass of wine in her hand. 'They need to laugh,' Rollo murmured. 'It's part of human nature; when something too awful to contemplate happens the old adage really works, "laughter is the best medicine".' In trying to prove his point he cynically added 'that is of course unless you have diabetes.'

Kitty stifled a giggle. 'Oh Rollo, you're a marvel; right as always. My mother-in-law has already had a go at me about the choice of music.'

'At least it was Jeff Buckley's version and not Leonard Cohen. Look Kitty, it doesn't mean we aren't all grieving for Tom but everyone is still profoundly shocked over his death and nobody really knows how to cope.'

'I know. I don't know whether I'm coming or going. Ever since the inquest opened I've found myself doing unnecessary jobs so I had no time to think. Yesterday I tidied the children's rooms twice as if it was the most important thing in the world to get their storybooks in alphabetical order. I found myself in floods of tears when I found Midge had put *The Gruffalo* with the *Alfie* stories.'

Kitty took a long slurp of wine. 'I really need this but please don't give me another until it is all over.'

5

'A word if you please, Mrs Munroe,' a large lady confronted Kitty, outrage oozing out of every pore. 'You said just finger food, cold meats, salads and little cakes but now, it seems now we need dishes and spoons. If you'd said you wanted puddings we would have provided them and set out the necessary implements as well.'

'I'm so sorry Mrs Finchcock. I didn't know anything about the fruit salad until a moment ago. My sister-in-law brought it. I'm very sorry for the inconvenience; I'll just go and find the bowls for you.'

The expression of righteous rage softened to one of sympathy and understanding. 'Don't fret yourself my dear, I'll find them. I'll go and get the bowls.' What could you say? Relax, enjoy yourself, laugh and be merry after all it's only your husband's funeral. Overcome by the awfulness of the situation Mrs Finchcock hurried back to her team of helpers in the kitchen.

'Who was that?'

Kitty giggled. 'That was the amazing Mrs Finchcock. She thinks she rules the village and everyone in it. Everyone is absolutely terrified of her and we all jump - when she says jump. The WI, Harvest Festival, the church flower rota, whatever's happening you can bet that Mrs Finchcock is chivvying everyone and everything along. She scared me stiff when we first came here; forcing me to 'do' flowers for the church, bake for the Brownies and ...'

'Kitty, as I recall you're the world's worst with flowers. What did you do?'

'I sneaked into Ashbourne and bought an arrangement from a flower shop. But don't tell anyone as everyone thinks I'm a floral whizz-kid.' Kit took another sip of her wine. 'Mrs Finchcock is terrifying but she is well intentioned and very kind. The day after Tom's,' Kitty's voice faltered and she took several deep breaths before continuing. 'She cycled up here with a fruit loaf and a bottle of her homemade elderflower cordial. She tidied the place up, the washing up, the laundry – everything.

'After the inquest had opened, and the County coroner had set the later date, she insisted that the WI ladies would provide the funeral tea. I told her that the funeral director had recommended some caterers but she wouldn't have any of it. Apparently, at times like this "village folk stick together" and although we are newcomers we're included.'

Roland put his arm around Kit and gave her a squeeze. 'That sounds like something out of a 1940s musical, *"Territory folk should stick together, territory folk should all be pals"*,' Roland's strong bass made some of the guests turn which made Kit giggle which again caused a few raised eyebrows and disapproving stares from a posse of her mother-in-law's bridge friends.

6

Rollo immediately looked chastened. 'They think we're behaving without proper decorum, so Mrs Munroe I'm going to circulate with some of this excellent Rioja and I advise you to go into the garden and find some agreeable company. Sue and Mike are out there.'

Taking Rollo's advice Kitty went through the front porch into the garden. This part of the garden looked lovely. Mrs Finchcock's influence had spread beyond the cold salmon and chicken salad as she'd commandeered several of the village husbands to trim the shrubs, mow the lawns and tidy the borders.

Sue and Mike and a group of friends were sitting on the bench under a rose pergola teeming with creamy white roses. Kitty was relieved to see them although she knew they would have moved heaven and earth not to leave her in the lurch on this awful day and after all she had been staying with them when she heard about Tom's accident.

In spite of their sincere smiles and murmured reassurances Kitty just wished that she could just turn the clock back and that the last fifteen months had never happened.

**** **** ****

Chapter 1

Life at Stoney Lea

Moving In

Tom, Kitty, three year old Sasha and two year old Midge moved into Stoney Lea farmhouse on a breezy early March day fifteen months ago.

Kitty hadn't taken Tom seriously when he first talked about moving to the country. It was true their pretty, little house had seemed cramped since baby Oliver, known as Midge had arrived. The points in favour of Tom's argument was that his job had changed and he frequently had more than an eighty mile round trip for work and he knew that Kitty wanted at least one more child and their current house was barely big enough for the four of them.

The extra space from an earlier kitchen extension and the addition of a conservatory were now inadequate as toys, pushchairs and sundry other pieces of child rearing equipment filled the once seemingly roomy space.

On the plus side they had a good and, above all, happy life in an upmarket, trendy Cheshire town and in Kitty's opinion, it seemed a shame to disrupt everything by moving away from friends, good schools and everything that was dear and familiar.

Kitty didn't mind the occasional game of tennis or even a gentle cycle ride and she would gladly join her friends for a pushchair trundle along the towpath. But she'd never had the enthusiasm or the inclination to keep up with her husband's more energetic activities.

Shortly after Kitty met Tom she discovered that if she intended to be part of his life she had to accept that she'd be spending her weekends cold and more often than not muddy or listening in thrall as Tom explained in detail the distinctions between various classic cars. Tom loved being out of doors - anything to take him away from his workplace. And now he was pressuring Kitty to uproot the family and move away from the security of their friends to take on a new life in an unknown and strange environment and in Kitty's mind, among bucolic eccentrics and rustic weirdos.

Country living, she was sure, would mean that she'd be forever in wellingtons and dungarees, up to the knees in pigswill and chicken feathers. The children would immediately be turned into country bumpkins dressed in homespun smocks with clogs on their feet. There would be no central heating and the hot water would have to be boiled in a cauldron after buckets of water had been heaved up from a well together with a selection of newts and toads. To reach the loo you'd need to trudge to the end of a yard knee-deep in indescribable muck.

Tom had laughed outright at Kitty's fears of having to don wellies every time she wanted to step out of the door and, although she might have to learn how to cook on an Aga, he promised the house would have all the mod cons she was used to.

On top of this being away from all the traffic and pollution would be so much better for the children. Midge already had several bronchial infections.

What Tom wanted was a house with outbuildings and some land. It had to be near a village and ideally not too far from a town with good transport links, as he would sometimes need to go to London, or further afield, for work. A village with a school, shop, church and pub where there would be some social life and they could become part of the community. It would be a house with character which they could work on to make their own; neither a mansion nor a cottage but somewhere big enough for them to welcome family and friends and somewhere where they could grow old together.

For once Kitty wouldn't let herself be convinced by Tom's persuasive arguments nor would she agree to look online or at any of brochures from estate agents, or the copies of *Country Life* which began arriving. Instead she involved herself in the community by going on the mother and toddlers committee and beginning a ruthless reorganisation of the children's rooms and the living room so it looked as if the house was not crowded and over cluttered.

On Kitty's birthday Tom organised a surprise childfree weekend in a luxurious country house hotel. It was after she had been lulled into a false sense of security by being cosseted in the hotel's spa, wined and dined in a Michelin starred restaurant and thoroughly made loved to in a massive four poster bed that Tom drove her through the pretty Staffordshire village of Eden Bridge. They continued along a winding, tree lined lane until, at a quarter to three, they arrived in the front yard of Stoney Lea Farm.

At first Kitty thought they had come to buy apples, as the orchard was full of laden fruit trees, but it was soon made clear that they were there with the intention to 'view the property'.

Kitty and Tom walked in from the yard straight into the farm's kitchen as in the country the front door, by tradition, is only used to welcome in a bride, a new baby or to carry out a coffin.

The flagstoned kitchen was huge. There was no other word for it. In the inglenook on the left hand side stood a dark blue Aga and on either side blue and white willow pattern plates were displayed on two Welsh oak dressers. Pinned to a beam on the far wall above a massive chest of drawers were rows of red rosettes and photographs of prize cattle and Shire horses. Almost filling the whole length of the room was a wide, well-scrubbed deal table.

Although the two cats sleeping in an intertwined heap in front of the Aga ignored the visitors a brown and white collie came forward with a waving plume of a tail to greet them.

'Gyp! Down! He means no harm. Mr and Mrs Munroe? Welcome to Stoney Lea Farm. I'm Dora Redman. You're a tad early. The agent isn't here yet as she told me you'd be arriving at three thirty. But I can show you round if that's all right.'

By the time the little red sports car of the estate agent turned into the yard Kitty's mind was made up; Stoney Lea Farm would be their future home.

As the farmland and the barns were being sold to neighbouring Manor Farm the sale would just include the house, some stone buildings in the farmyard, a small back yard, some outbuildings and a bothy in the walled gardens, with greenhouses, orchards and the home paddock; nearly six and a half acres in all. Tom had never envisaged himself as a farmer so the extent and acreage of the property suited him. Kitty was so entranced with everything that she took in very little of what the agent or Mrs Redman were saying.

She grasped the fact that the kitchen dressers, chest of drawers and the table were part of the fixtures as were the cupboards in the scullery, the old dairy, washhouse and storerooms. The oak corner cupboards in the sitting room and dining room were being left as well. The kitchen table was too large to move as years ago it had been assembled in the kitchen and to remove it would mean destroying it or knocking down a wall. All she could think of was how marvellous it would be if they could be in the house for Christmas. It wasn't to be.

Christmas and New Year were over before everything was signed and sealed and they were organised, packed up and ready to move from suburban

10

Cheshire to rural Staffordshire. In spite of an enormous stroke of luck due to the quick sale of their own house what with all the rigmarole and endless telephone calls and emails to the solicitors, surveyors, estate agents and a lengthy niggle between the solicitors over a right of way across the home paddock it was early March before they finally moved in.

It was when the furniture vans had lumbered out of the yard and some essentials had been unpacked from the dozens of boxes and the children were busily introducing their favourite toys to their new home that the real work begun.

Over the next few weeks hordes of visitors turned up; eager to see the new house and with offers to help, hinder or just to offer useless comments or criticism.

Kitty's parents were the first to appear.

George and Betty Oxley arrived armed with bottles of chilled champagne, orange juice and packets of jammy dodgers for the children, extra milk, bread, butter and mustard and a large joint of cold roast beef; ready for action with their work clothes, a bag of useful tools, a set of ladders and a vast quantity of dust sheets.

Although they had already seen round the house the full tour took some time as it involved a detailed description of plans for new bathrooms and renovating the old washhouse into an office for Tom and refitting the array of pantries, storerooms and larders which surrounded the scullery into a working kitchen and utility room. Both Kitty and Tom had agreed to keep the farmhouse kitchen exactly as it was.

Their first priority was to repaint the children's bedrooms. The house had two large bedrooms and two smaller ones. The bathroom was currently off the scullery. Over the big kitchen was an enormous room that the Redman's had used as a storeroom. Years ago farm labourers would have slept in there. It had its own hidden staircase behind a door in the kitchen as well as access from the upstairs landing. At the moment it was the second warmest room in the house and the whole family were sleeping in it.

Betty Oxley loved the house but had some reservations. 'Kit, you are going to rattle around in this big place!'

'It certainly seems a lot bigger than it was when the Redmans were here and our sweet little sofas look lost in the sitting room but we'll manage. The room above the kitchen will be our room. We thought at first in letting the children have it but it's such a great space. We're going to knock through to over the scullery and put in a bathroom. Built in wardrobes will be under the sloping ceiling. For the time being Tom will have his 'office' at the other end. Midge is having the bigger of the two little rooms as Sasha has chosen the room looking over the orchard. We're going to knock through and put in a guest bathroom in the box room and one for the children in the other little bedroom as soon as we can. So the only rooms we're going to redecorate for the moment are the children's so they will be ready for them once the central heating has been installed.'

At three-and-a-half, Sasha was going through a pink 'princess' stage and to Kitty's delight and relief her mother persuaded her granddaughter to choose the softer seashell shades on the paint chart rather than the bright candyfloss hues she had previously favoured.

Whereas Kitty's parents had literally rolled up their sleeves and knuckled down to help wherever they could Tom's family had a very different approach. The move had brought Tom and Kitty nearer to his family. His parents and brother now lived less than ten miles away.

On the second Sunday after the move Ted and Simone Munroe arrived at twelve forty five for a one o'clock lunch together with a bottle of champagne that needed chilling and a huge bouquet of flowers. Complaining about the mud and muck, which had splattered their car at what became known as Cowpat Corner, Simone insisted Kitty immediately found suitable vases so the flowers could be arranged.

Kitty cursed her mother-in-law, as she had to leave the first proper meal she'd cooked on the Aga to find them.

Kitty was terrified of the Aga and all it represented. Too Jilly Cooperish or *The Archers* she thought. Some of her friends had raved about them, saying how easy it was to use and how so little could go wrong. Others had shaken their heads and muttered stories of culinary disasters with overcooked and inedible meals.

Although the Aga was somewhat elderly it was in full working order and Mrs Redman had run over the basics with her and left some pages of notes and handy hints. But a full Sunday lunch for her mother and father-in-law was an ordeal that she'd hoped to delay.

So far they'd managed with bacon and eggs, pasta and anything else that could be cooked and simmered on the hob. Today's menu was simple enough; a leg of lamb, roast potatoes, carrots, peas and apple crumble and custard. A meal Kit had cooked dozens of times before, albeit on a traditional cooker.

Tom and his father went off to tour the outbuildings as he had plans to change the old cart shed into a workshop. Just like his father, Tom had always loved cars. While Kitty and the children and their accumulated collection of toys, sweet wrappers and shopping bags were confined to a reliable medium sized people carrier Tom drove a two-seater Porsche N11.

Stoney Lea Farm's outbuildings guaranteed that there was plenty of secure space to fulfil his lifelong ambition of renovating and restoring a classic car.

Ted Munroe was just as enthusiastic about the scheme. Semi-retired he had time on his hands and he could see the advantage of having a workshop and all the associated disorder away from his own house and his fastidious wife. There would be plenty of room at Stoney Lea Farm to house his current project thus freeing up his own garage.

Simone Munroe, insisting that Sasha helped her to arrange the flowers, monopolised the scullery as the deep crimson roses and pale oriental lilies were cut and placed in the vases. Simone deplored Kitty's lack of an oasis to hold the flowers in place or the correct size of vase to show the blooms to their full advantage. Sasha stuck a lily and a piece of the discarded purple ribbon behind her ear and decided that today she would be a flower fairy princess.

Meanwhile, in the kitchen Kitty was going slowly round the bend. The lamb was more than ready and rested, the roast potatoes were crisp but rather than golden they were becoming to resemble lumps of coal and the vegetables, which should have been the easiest part of the meal, were still nowhere near ready.

Mrs Redman had warned her that when the ovens were busy the hob was often much slower than usual. On top of this Kitty had made the typical mistake of new Aga cooks by leaving the hob lids open after she'd boiled the kettle for coffee at eleven o'clock. This meant a lot of precious heat had been wasted. There was no easy back up, as they hadn't replaced the microwave, which had been built into the kitchen in their old house.

The peas were easier to deal with as Kitty kept on boiling her old electric kettle and changing the water. The same process wasn't as successful with the carrots, which remained rock hard.

By the time Tom and his father had washed their hands, the flowers arranged to Simone's exacting standards, Kitty had set the table, woken Midge from his morning nap and had drunk two glasses of wine. This had better be just Sunday lunch for the in-laws nerves, she thought as she topped up her glass rather than an Aga related thing.

13

Kitty had cause to be anxious as the lamb had by now shrunk to half its original size with all the pink juiciness obliterated and the potatoes could easily pass as nutty slack. Nearly all the colour had leached out of the peas while the carrots were still as solid as mosaic tiles. When she'd gone to skim the fat off the gravy she had been so distracted by the clutter of cellophane, shredded florist ribbon, bits of discarded stems and unwanted foliage left in the scullery that she had poured the gravy down the sink instead.

This first roast Sunday lunch in their new home therefore couldn't be said to be a success. Simone turned her elegant nose up at the leathery looking slices of lamb that Tom placed on her plate. She refused the peas and potatoes and looked in vain for the gravy.

Ted and Tom, really hungry by now, wolfed up their meat and vegetables without really tasting them but the rock hard potatoes defeated them. Midge, at times a fussy eater, spooned up the meat, peas and carrots as if his mother had presented him with a plate of the god's ambrosia. The apple crumble was a trifle crusty though edible but due to the three glasses of wine Kitty had forgotten to make the custard.

The champagne, now adequately chilled, helped to make up for the inadequacies of the meal. 'To Tom, Kitty, Sasha and Midge – much happiness at Stoney Lea Farm!' toasted a beaming Ted.

Here it comes, thought Kitty as Simone raised her glass. The name that no one has ever used – not even that vile geography teacher.

'Yes, to dearest Tom, Sasha, dear little Midge and Kathryn good luck in your new house,' echoed Simone, who in spite of claiming that she 'hardly ate a thing' was starving after the unpalatable lunch. She decided that they'd leave after coffee and call in on her eldest son and her highly organised daughter-in-law for an early afternoon tea.

If Simone hadn't been so eager to be off and to also miss the washing up she would have been able to enjoy a lavish and delicious tea with Tom and Kitty.

When Tom's brother Christopher and Melissa, his wife and their children had visited the farmhouse they too had come laden with "fizz" and a huge gourmet hamper full of extravagant treats. This was indeed welcome although Kitty suspected that it was a leftover Christmas hamper from her sister-in-law's business. The holly motif on some of the items and a supermarket pack of long grain rice squashed into a Christmas pudding shaped hole had rather given it away.

Melissa Munroe was a successful businesswoman in her own right. She ran a consultancy agency for, as far as Kitty could make out, businessmen – she

14

referred to as team captains in the software industry who considered themselves too important to think of things for themselves. She also had a smattering of football players and to a lesser extent some minor TV celebrities with not enough time on their hands. Naturally, they preferred to pay huge sums of money for Melissa and her team to do it for them. In essence she was like a real life major domo or *Siri* come to life.

Her success meant that she often needed to travel to deal with her client's needs and therefore delegated great portions of her domestic life to other people such as: decorators, cleaners, gardeners, ironing ladies, caterers and to a large extent parenting. Dominic and Tristan Munroe had spent more of their seven years with nannies and au pairs than they had with their parents.

Although Melissa preferred a minimalist style of living she couldn't help admiring the old farmhouse and saw its potential as a stylish residence or for a hefty fee a film location. Her sister-in-law's plans for turning it into a family home didn't really interest her but she was voluble in offering suggestions for modernising and 'improving' the place.

Her sharp eyes missed nothing from the wide oak floorboards in the sitting and dining rooms to the row of jugs on the mantle over the Aga. 'Kitty, since when have you collected Clarice Cliff?'

'Oh, the jugs, the Redmans left them. They were in one of the corner cupboards.'

'Left them? They must be worth a bomb!'

'If only. There's a crack in the middle sized one and a tiny chip on the rim of the big one but I think the little one is perfect. I rang Mrs Redman and she told me that whatever they'd left they didn't want. They were her mother-in-law's and as she'd never liked Clarice Cliff and no one else in her family wanted them. She insisted that anything we found we were to consider as ours. She is delighted with her new bungalow and looking forward to treating herself to some new furniture so the Clarice Cliff stays at Stoney Lea Farm.'

'Have they left anything else of value?'

'I don't think so. There are some oddments of crockery and iron saucepans and a few old dishes and a couple of ewers from old bedroom jug and basin sets, no chamber pots though, nothing really special. Tom has found some ancient garden tools, a hand plough and an enormous wheelbarrow but that's about it.'

'Sounds as if they've left you country living on a plate.' Commonplace rural artefacts weren't of interest to Melissa's mercenary mind and she began looking around in case there were other treasures her sister-in-law had

15

unknowingly missed. But apart from the kitchen and the large bedroom the house was cold and the scullery on that February afternoon quite glacial.

Melissa then began on another tack. 'I suppose when you're a little more settled you'll be thinking about going back to work. I've forgotten what you did as it's so long since you had a job but I'm sure there's something around here that would suit your abilities and limited qualifications.'

What a prize bitch, Kitty thought. For years she'd been aware that her sister-in-law held a poor opinion of her capabilities but even so she was taken aback by Melissa's direct and downright insulting opinion of her professional abilities.

'When you do get your act together I can put you in touch with an excellent au pair agency. I've used it for all my girls and we've never been disappointed.'

I wonder if Dominic and Tristan would agree with that, thought Kitty. She knew from the last time the twins had stayed with them they still had bedwetting problems.

'It could be a difficulty getting someone to take you on as you're out in the sticks,' Melissa continued. 'Anyone worthwhile would need her own car of course but that big room over the kitchen could be turned into a flat and if you ... '

'Thanks for the offer, Mel but Kitty is going to remain a stay-at-home mum; that's right isn't it darling?' Kitty felt Tom's protective arm around her shoulder and all her inadequacies, magnified by being left alone for over half an hour with her sister-in-law, disappeared. 'There are loads for her to do here even after we've got the house sorted. Kitty will become the envy of the village when she wins all the prizes at the village fête with her homemade jam, pickled plums and the wonkiest looking vegetables. You're going to be the earth mother to beat all earth mothers isn't that right darling?'

Kit wasn't sure about this. It was true that she was itching to have a go at producing some of their own food but 'earth mother' that was too close to the children wearing homespun smocks and clogs and the dungarees and wellington image that Tom had reassured her would never be part of their new life.

She smiled up at both Tom and Melissa. 'We'll have to see what happens when Sasha and Midge have started school but I can see that the house will keep me busy and out of mischief for a long time.'

16

'Oh Kitty!' shrieked her sister-in-law. 'You getting into mischief!' Melissa's diamond encrusted hand patted Kitty's arm. "You are such an innocent and far too placid and easy going for all that!'

Luckily Midge rushed in wailing that Dominic was strangling his teddy bear. Kitty swept him up before she had chance to show Melissa just how wrong she was in her judgement of her sister-in-law's character.

Chapter 2

Settling In

On reflection the first year at Stoney Lea Farm was a happy one. Initially it was a busy time which merged for Kitty, into a procession of meetings with architects and planning officials, making endless cups of tea to keep the builders going and on top of all this finding out that she was loving country and, especially village life.

Once the central heating had been installed the confusion in the rest of the house became bearable. The architect's enthusiasm and the potential it offered rubbed off on to both Kitty and Tom so that the simplicity of their original plans gradually expanded. An upstairs bathroom and an en suite for a guest room remained the same. But the plans for the built-in wardrobes in their room over the kitchen became a walk-in dressing room with Velux windows to give more light and, if sun tunnel windows were installed, the bathroom could become a wet room. All the fixtures and fittings were, of course to be the height of quality and style.

Unfortunately their finances for the project had to be drastically changed as Tom had bought a Range Rover 4.6L to be delivered the day after they'd moved in. Naturally it was a classic. No way was he going to buy a Range Rover Sport. From Tom's point of view it was a necessary part of country living as there would be extreme winter weather to negotiate and most likely, later on, a pony trailer to tow.

Kitty's argument was that the local paper would be full of second hand vehicles and that they had months to go before the next winter. She felt that every penny should go on their "nest" and that it didn't matter what they drove as long as it went and they could get from A to B in safety.

Tom's claim was that he had got a very good price for his two year old Porsche N11 and that he worked bloody hard and therefore could spend his bonus anyway he damn well liked.

But the Range Rover – with its headlights splattered with from driving round Cowpat Corner and Tom's flat cap casually left on the passenger seat and one of his newly acquired waxed jackets and green Hunter wellingtons in the boot

– must have triggered some guilt because as a concession, he sold his beloved 1953 split screen Morris Minor.

That six thousand pounds ensured the central heating was installed and the structural work for the children's bathroom and the guest en suite begun but after that everything else was left in limbo until either the next tranche of bonuses arrived or there was a windfall from some miraculous source or other.

Initially, while Kitty was getting used to country living she found she was missing her circle of friends; some, like Sue and Mike, stretched back to her school days.

Sue, Mike and their children had driven over to stay for the weekend but Kitty felt a yawning gap and a strange feeling of bereavement as they waved them goodbye on the Sunday evening.

So, it had been a welcome surprise the next morning to find a tall, dark haired woman and a small boy on their doorstep.

The woman was wearing a red velvet jacket, flowing black trousers anchored at the ankles by bicycle clips and a black woolly hat festooned with red and purple felt anemones.

The boy looked to be about the same age as Sasha. He too was clothed in bright clothing; vivid blue dungarees, a hand knitted jacket displaying dancing green and blue elephants while black curls stuck out from under a stripy hat complete with earflaps and tiger's ears.

'Hi. We thought we call by to welcome you to Stoney Lea. We're your nearest neighbours. Xavier and I live up the lane in The Goat Shed.'

'You live with goats?' asked a curious Sasha; abandoning playing fighting farmers with Midge and an assortment of plastic animals.

Midge pushed under her mother's arm to find out whom she was talking to.

'Not with goats,' their visitor laughed. 'The official name is Rose Cottage but for centuries it has housed domesticated animals. The last inhabitants before it was turned into a rural des-res were a herd of champion British Toggenburg goats. There's a lot of people round here with long memories and so the Goat Shed has stuck.'

'We don't mind as goats are nice,' the boy informed Sasha. 'Tilda and Drusilla live in part of our garden and we drink their milk.'

Sasha was intrigued. 'You get milk from goats?'

The boy nodded. 'Come and see them.'

'Now?'

'That's why we've called round to see if you'd like to come over.'

19

Kitty was dumbstruck. 'Hang on a minute while we get our coats.'

That first morning of coffee and chat in the Goat Shed's cosy living room, while the children played, was the first of many. In Izzie Buchann, Kitty rapidly found a true friend, as she was a sympathetic listener, a keeper of secrets with good common sense as well as being great fun to be with.

Izzie seemed to know the right time to turn up and whisk Sasha and Midge away when Stoney Lea was knee deep in electricians or so that Tom and Kitty's lengthy discussions with the architect could be without childish interruptions. She introduced Kitty to the ins and outs of village life including footpaths and shortcuts and to other mums and their children.

For all her friendliness and generosity Izzie still retained a mystique, which as Kitty discovered provided plentiful speculation for the local gossips.

Xavier was an easy going little boy and to Kitty, he didn't seem to have any hang-ups or problems. His mother's philosophy was, that as long as you respected yourself and others and added to the common good whenever possible life was there to be lived and enjoyed.

Kitty wholeheartedly went along with this. As her friendship with Izzie grew closer there remained a degree of reserve between Izzie and Tom who referred to her as Kitty's arty-farty pal or made oblique references to lesbian and leftie leanings.

It was true Izzie was out-spoken and dressed in a bohemian way. She made all her and Xavier's clothes as well as the soft furnishings and quilts scattered throughout their house. She also seemed impervious to Tom's charms. Kitty, disregarding Tom's taunts, recognised the intellectual, creative and overall kind woman behind the somewhat alternative lifestyle.

Tom half-heartedly accepted some of Izzie's advice when it came to cultivating and planting out the vegetable beds. She'd recommended planting and harvesting crops according to the lunar calendar, which Kitty was keen to go along with it and Tom ignored. After flicking through a couple of gardening books, Tom took over working in the vegetable garden with enthusiasm and as his knowledge grew he became very protective of his domain. However, during their first harvest he was the first to admit that Izzie's carrots were bigger and tastier than the ones he'd grown in Stoney Lea's vegetable garden.

Their other close neighbours were separated from Stoney Lea by the home paddock. Beth and Mark Willoughby and their two children lived at Manor Farm. Mark was a huge, gentle giant of a man who had inherited and now farmed one of the biggest farms in the neighbourhood but there was nothing of the typical farmer's wife in Beth.

She was petite and dainty with naturally fair hair and cornflower blue eyes. Beth's dazzling looks belied her sunny disposition, practical nature and genuine kindness. Even in a simple T-shirt, old jeans and wellingtons - albeit green ones - she looked as if she had dressed for a smart, social occasion and not about to go out and dig up spuds in the farm's vegetable garden.

Whereas Tom's dislike of Izzie was palpable he heartily approved of Mark recognising the drive and determination to succeed that was in his own character. But while Tom revelled in social situations Mark was at heart a stay-at-home, family man who, apart from events which involved the whole village tolerated Beth's kitchen supper parties out of his great love for his wife.

What had also helped Kitty to settle in to her new life was that Sasha and Midge immediately became best friends with Xavier and with Alice and Harry, Beth and Mark's two children. Sasha, Alice and Xavier were close in age and would all start school together in September. Midge was just a few months older than Harry. All five children played together happily in any one of the three houses while their mothers chatted, drank coffee and at times helped each other out with child minding.

Chapter 3

Girl's Talk

'Is this decadence or just plain indulgence?'

Kitty concentrated. She was lying on a plaid rug in Manor Farm's orderly garden while Beth and Izzie lounged on the cushions on a silvered-oak bench. The flush of the red and orange streaked evening sky had finally changed into navy blue and was being lit by the first faint stars. Kitty could see bats sweeping overhead and the silhouettes of a pair of owls hunting over the nearby fields.

What had initially started as an impromptu children's tea party had turned into a sleepover. Upstairs, in Beth and Mark's huge, king-sized bed Xavier, Sasha and Midge were finally asleep curled up beside Alice and Harry.

'I think it is indulgence as we're not depraved, debauched or dissipated,' was her final decision.

'Speak for yourself,' Izzie poured herself another margarita from the jug. 'I have been all three in my time. This is the reformed Izzie Buchann you see before you. The old Isabel Blakeney would have been dancing on the table by now surrounded by hordes of gorgeous *hombres* all begging for her favours.'

'Blakeney – not Buchann?'

'Buchann – Blakeney; who cares? It's just a name,' said Izzie.

'Where and when?' asked Beth as she refilled Kitty's glass. 'Definitely not at a WI meeting with Mrs Finchcock's beady eye on you making sure everything is in order and all the cups are put away in the correct cupboard.'

'And the teaspoons are all accounted for,' added Kitty, taking a sip of her drink.

This really was very pleasant. Her initial disappointment that Tom was staying on for a couple of days in London after his business trip to Seattle had dissolved in Izzie and Beth's lively company. He had promised to be home on Friday night ready for the village fête on Saturday.

This would be their first real involvement in village life since they had moved to Stoney Lea. Their time so far had been dominated by waiting in for the heating engineer to turn up and decorating the children's bedrooms and the sitting room and dining room now that the central heating had been installed.

The plans for the scullery, their bedroom and installing the upstairs bathrooms were still on hold. This was a sore point with Kitty.

The reason for this was that a month after buying the Range Rover Tom and his father had gone to Birmingham to attend a business exhibition. Kitty later realised this was a trumped up excuse to go on an extravagant spending-spree.

After two days Tom and Ted Munroe returned in high, slightly inebriated spirits; jubilant that Tom had managed to purchase, at a truly "bargain price" the classic car of his dreams; a four-gear 1937 Jackson-Johnson.

To the casual observer the dilapidated vehicle with its torn hide seats and scratched dark blue paintwork was not impressive. When Tom proudly informed his stunned wife to observe the echoes of a Bugatti in the way the bodywork tapered into an elegant boat-tailed rear Kitty had difficulty making out this outstanding feature amongst the battered and dented bodywork.

Nor did her father-in-law's admission that, although it would need a complete engine re-build as well as the necessary cosmetic repairs and renovations, in a couple of years or so between them they would have the Jackson-Johnson in prime condition ready for road or competition use. Ted Munroe was confident that Tom had got himself a fantastic opportunity. There was work to be done but between them it was possible and, after all there was excellent workshops and storage facilities at Stoney Lea.

Tom was convinced that the car was destined for him. By coincidence - there was the number plate to start with TDM; his initials followed by his birth date 719, albeit in the American style. He was thoroughly aware that he would have to work really hard to placate Kitty before she could be persuaded that the car's purchase had been right for them. He knew it had totally blown their budget out of the water for completing the renovations but surely loads of other families managed with just one bathroom.

Tom did his best to win Kitty round. He'd returned home with flowers and two bottles of her favourite champagne. But as they hadn't had the positive effect he'd hoped for, he offered to feed their newly acquired hens and the children and put both commodities to bed while she had a bath.

Later, after he'd admitted to her exactly how much he'd spent on that "pile of junk" did Kitty really erupt. Her anger and disappointment made Tom fully realise that it would need a lot more than a couple of bottles of fizz, throwing corn for chickens and cooking a tray of oven fries and fish fingers to get back in her good books.

In spite of the beauty of the summer evening and the margaritas Tom's treachery still rankled. Not only had it pushed back their plans for the house but also the wretched car was draining away whatever savings they would otherwise put aside towards finishing the bathrooms and bedrooms.

As each week went by Tom or his father were either spending hours online tracking down the specialist pieces necessary for the rebuild or showing the heap of junk to fellow classic car enthusiasts who, as if by magic, found their way to Stoney Lea's yard to ogle the wreck. The children were seeing less of their father as Tom was spending most of the weekends and the long summer evenings at the workbench or in his greasy, oily overalls under the car.

Midge had been banned from the workshop after he'd picked up an interesting looking piece of metal and a few screws but forgot where he'd left them. When Sasha was allowed to watch her daddy working she got oil on her new shoes, which transferred on to the leather seats. Kitty was still not sure who was the more upset; Tom because of the oil stains on the ancient upholstery or Sasha because her pretty, sparkly party shoes were ruined.

When a kettle, mugs and a small fridge were installed in the workshop the family saw even less of each other.

Having left their sleeping children in Beth and Mark's bed Kitty stood at Stoney Lea's gate and watched Izzie walk up the lane towards the Goat Shed.

It had only been a few weeks after they'd moved in that they had decided to drop 'Farm' and just call their new home Stoney Lea after a number of seed reps and corn merchants came cold calling and left after cups of tea and shortbread, disappointed they'd failed to drum up business from the new owners.

One of these days, Kitty thought as she opened the kitchen door, she'd find out which field was the designated stony one. Apart from their paddock the land surrounding the house were now part of Manor Farm and filled with Mark's placid black and white cows grazing on the lush green grass. Sleeping on the gentle lower slopes of the Hatherstone Hills were his flocks of black faced sheep and their lambs. Kitty knew it was one of Midge's dearest wishes to go with Mark and his two Border collies, Spark and Billy on the quad bike when he went to check the sheep.

Inside the kitchen the phone was ringing.

'Kitty? Is that you? Where the hell have you been? I've been ringing you all evening.'

'Hello Tom, I was with Izzie …'

'I might have known – the village's liberated lesbian leading you astray – again,' said Tom in his most disparaging tone.

'Tom, we were with the kids at Beth and Mark's.'

'Kitty, what are you thinking of? It's a week day!'

'They are fast asleep at Beth's. Mark will drop them off tomorrow – in time for nursery school.'

'I still think it's irresponsible of you.'

Kitty sighed. 'Tom, you know we've done it before.'

There was a low chuckle on the other end of the phone, 'Oh yes, I remember. We had the whole house to ourselves. Wish I was home right now – eh Kit-Kat?'

'I can't promise that the house will be as empty tomorrow but, I guarantee that I'll be very pleased to see you.' Kitty paused. 'What time do you expect to be home?'

'Oh Kitty, that's what I was ringing about. I won't be back tomorrow. Something's come up so I've got to go to … Zurich.'

"Zurich? Why?'

'There's been a bit of a crisis and I've got to sort things out. I'll be back by Sunday.'

'But it's the village fête!'

'I know. I'm absolutely gutted. I'll be back as soon as I can. Tell the kids I'm sorry and will make it up to them. I must go. Bye. Love you.'

'Tom? Tom?' But the line was dead and when she tried to ring him back Tom's phone was turned off. Straight to voicemail.

Chapter 4

After the Fête

'Mummy! Uncle Chris' car is in the yard.'

'Shit!' Kitty was still recovering from the village fête. Not only had she helped to set up and clear away but she'd been on a stall almost single-handed because Tom was in bloody Zurich instead of handing out tombola prizes. Thank goodness her mum and dad looked after the children supplying them with candyfloss, hot dogs and pony rides as well as helping behind the stall so she could nip to the loo. The Rector and his wife had also taken turns rolling the tombola drum for her and matching tickets to prizes.

Today she'd hoped for a more relaxed time but now her brother-in-law and his twin sons had turned up.

'Hello Kitty, hello Sasha,' called Chris opening the car's rear doors so his sons could make their escape. 'We thought we'd come over as Melissa is still away on a business trip. Boys, say hello to Auntie Kitty.'

Dominic and Tristan mumbled something that could be deciphered as a greeting before rushing off towards the front garden.

'Sasha? Where's Midge? Midge, your cousins are in the garden – play nicely.' Kitty forced herself to smile, 'Would you like a coffee Chris?'

'Thanks, that would be great but a beer would be even better.'

Beer, thought Kitty - that means he intends stopping.

'Just what the doctor ordered,' grinned Chris drowning half the can in a couple of gulps. 'Childcare is such hard work.'

'How long has Melissa been away?'

'Since Tuesday, I expected her back on Friday but something came up that needed her particular attention. I can cope OK during the week as the boys are at school and the au pair is around. But today is Viktoria's day off.'

Oho! So that's it, thought Kitty before wiping resentment aside. 'Would you like to stay for lunch?'

'Thanks Kit, that would be great,' grinned Chris finishing his beer.

The day hadn't been so bad, thought Kitty as she stacked the dishwasher. Only two of the sweet pea tepees had been demolished and Dominic would only have mild bruising, as Chris had been really quick getting the croquet mallet off Tristan.

Midge and Sasha, still tired from the excitement of the fête hadn't enjoyed sharing Sunday and their mother with their cousins. Given the slightest opportunity the seven-year-old boys teased and tormented Midge while regarding Sasha as just 'a soppy girl'. So there'd been tears and squabbles and a lot of 'not fair' from all parties. Chris hadn't helped by taking himself off and leaving her to keep the peace while he tinkered with the Jackson-Johnson in the workshop. Even Chris wasn't foolish enough to let his sons anywhere near such a valuable pile of scrap.

What does Melissa actually do? thought Kitty searching in the freezer for some bread for the morning. And what was it that was so urgent that it needed doing over the weekend instead of during the working week or online from home?

Kitty knew that part of her sister-in-law's business was to manage a series of properties. Her clients, according to Melissa, included some notable celebs, preferred staying in an apartment rather than in a hotel when they were in the country. This meant she was either viewing property, seeing designers and decorators in readiness for refurbishment or checking apartments for clients. All this kept her away from home a great deal, returning laden with extravagant guilt-gifts for her husband and her sons.

Tom often referred to her as 'a glorified concierge', which always made Kitty giggle as she imagined her glamorous sister-in-law, still in her spiky heels but dressed in an overall and headscarf plying a broom. Tom, she thought as she dragged the heavy wheelie bins through the moonlit yard to the gate, had better bring us home some extravagant presents to make up for the weekend and not just Toblerone or a fridge magnet of the Jungfrau.

27

Chapter 5

Chutney and Chat

Kitty pushed the heavy pan to the side of the hotplate and wiped her streaming eyes on a corner of her apron before answering the phone.

At least the caller wouldn't be able to smell the onions, garlic and vinegar, which for weeks had permeated the kitchen as well as her clothes and hair. The caller was Sue.

'Hello Kit, how are things? Still chopping away?'

"I certainly am. Apparently September and October is the chutney season here in the country and every kitchen for miles around reeks of vinegar.'

'But the end result will be worth it as you'll have all those jars of chutneys and pickles to last you throughout the winter.'

"There is that and the larder shelves look wonderful – a site to gladden the sight of the most stalwart WI member.'

'Even the formidable Mrs Finchcock?'

'Even Mrs Finchcock!' Kitty laughed. 'But this batch is definitely going to be the last lot - for this year anyway.'

'What is it?'

'Plum and apple – or rather apple and plum as we still have an enormous amount of apples.'

'Sounds lovely; please save a jar for me.'

'Will do.'

'So splashing out on a jam pan was worth it?'

Kitty laughed and pulled a wry face at the phone, 'This jam pan is going to the back of the deepest, darkest cupboard I can find until next year!'

'Didn't Izzie say that there'd be a late crop of raspberries?

'If there is we'll eat them or let the birds have them; I'm done for this year. Anyway, how are you? Are Lottie and Luke over the chickenpox?'

'They are fine; a bit spotty still but not contagious anymore so we'll be OK to come over for Bonfire Night.'

'Fantastic! I am really looking forward to seeing you all and the children are talking about it all the time and where you'll sleep.' Kitty paused. 'It is such a shame we haven't got the new bathrooms,'

'Still no progress?'

'No and there won't be for some time as there isn't any money.'

On the other end of the phone Sue frowned; there had been a note of despondency in her friend's voice that she hadn't heard before.

"It is that bloody car,' Kitty continued. 'Tom has had another rise and a mid-year bonus but it's already been spent.' Kitty tried but couldn't keep a petulant note out of her voice. 'He spends more time in the workshop than he does in the house. At the weekends the children hardly see him and all the work he initially put into the kitchen garden has gone by the board, as he says he hasn't the time or, obviously, the inclination. Any veg we've managed to produce is all due to Izzie as I've never grown anything except herbs or tomatoes before.'

'Won't things improve when it gets colder?'

'I doubt it. His dad turned up last week with a massive Calor Gas heater and he'd already bagged the little electric fan heaters we bought when we first moved in. He says it is really cosy out there.'

'Oh Kitty!' Sue and Mike had discussed the problems the Jackson-Johnson was causing at Stoney Lea. They both thought that Tom was being selfish and pig-headed in refusing George and Betty's offer of a loan to finish the bathrooms.

'He says that he's doing it for me and the children and when he sells it on we'll be rolling in money and we can have gold-plated taps if we want them - even in the yard.'

'Do you want gold-plated taps?'

'No!' Kitty laughed. 'Oh Sue, I am looking forward to seeing you. Apparently Bonfire Night is a big thing in Eden Bridge and people come from miles around. There'll be live music, jugglers, a barbeque and a beer tent as well as the bonfire and fireworks. Sasha wants to enter the best-dressed Guy competition and if you can come the day before there will be time for Lottie to help her stuff and dress it.'

'She'll like that. They are both really excited about seeing Sasha and Midge again.'

'Oh there's Beth's car in the yard. She's picked up Midge from playgroup so I must go. Speak again before you come to stay. Love to Mike and the kids. Bye.'

Aware the place still stank of vinegar and onions Kitty opened the kitchen door.

Midge staggered in carrying a huge marrow, which he heaved on to the kitchen table.

'Mrs Finchcock has given us this. She had five but I chose the biggest one.' Midge beamed at his mother for his own ingenuity.

'Mrs F says she'll let you have her recipe for marrow and ginger jam,' said Beth as she and Harry entered the kitchen. 'As it was one of Mrs Redman's specialities she thought you'd like to carry on the tradition,' Beth grinned, as she knew Kitty was fed up to the back teeth with making jam and chutneys.

'Oh no' groaned Kitty. 'I thought I had finished with all that for one year.'

'You'll have to make some as our beloved village matriarch will check up on you.'

'I know,' Kitty laughed. Maybe more chopping and simmering would sublimate some of the anger she felt towards Tom and that bloody car. 'Well, I'll need some more jars and Beth, do you fancy a glass of wine?'

Chapter 6

Lodgers

In early March Kitty and Tom invited the Goat Shed and Manor Farm families, Rollo and Kitty's parents for Sunday lunch and to celebrate their first year at Stoney Lea.

Kitty's attempt to make the lunch from their own produce was more or less successful - home grown potatoes, coleslaw from their own onions and red and white cabbages, eggs from the hens which clucked and pecked in the kitchen garden, a variety of homemade pickles, chutneys and a spicy cauliflower curry simmering on the hob.

Kitty and the Aga were now the best of friends so there were loaves of freshly baked bread and golden-crusted apple pies. The centrepiece was a gloriously, glazed ham courtesy of one of Manor Farm's porkers.

Izzie contributed goats' cheeses and yoghurt and Beth brought sponge cakes and meringues oozing with cream from the Manor Farm cows.

Gazing round the kitchen Kitty remembered the disastrous roast lamb lunch she'd made a year ago and the early baking attempts resulting in burnt and rock-hard biscuits and sagging, soggy cakes, which she'd produced in their first months at Stoney Lea.

Her mother must've been reading her mind as she came over and hugged her, 'Well done darling. Daddy and I are so proud of you.'

'What's that?' asked George coming over with a tankard of Mark's homebrewed beer.

'I was just saying how proud we are of Kitty and Tom and everything they've achieved.'

'We'd be prouder if the new bathrooms were finished,' commented George. 'Kitty, please have another go at getting Tom to accept a loan.'

'Dad, I've tried and tried until I'm bloody well fed up of trying. Anyway, if he did accept I bet the money would go straight on that blasted heap.' Kitty was cross with herself, she'd been determined that the Jackson-Johnson wouldn't spoil their celebration.

'I told you not to mention the bathrooms,' grumbled Betty as she dragged her husband away under the pretext of checking on the curry.

'Do you think that's why Tom's family aren't here,' asked George who had thought that the gathering comprised of rather a jolly crowd and up to then hadn't noticed that Tom's family were missing.

After the lunch while the children were watching a rowdy film the conversation in the kitchen came round to country living and the year's natural cycle.

'Farming is full of the unexpected and however much you plan there will always be something that can alter events and sometimes have long lasting effects,' Mark declared, spreading the last of the goats' cheese on to an oat biscuit.

'Like foot and mouth?' said George.

'Don't ever, ever mention it,' ordered Beth wagging her finger at George. 'But yes, things do happen and farmers have to cope with unforeseen disasters.'

'Three huge trees blew down in a tremendous storm the other year,' commented Izzie.

'And Prunehill lost their barn roof,' added Mark.

'No one could get up or down the lane,' Izzie continued. 'Until they were cleared – the milk tanker, the post van. Everything.'

'But we all had enough logs to last us all winter and beyond,' laughed Mark. 'Now, my present problem is that lambing has started and the ewes are dropping their lambs at breakneck speed and some of the theaves are just not coping with their youngsters.'

'Theaves?' queried Betty.

'The first time mums are known as theaves and only become ewes once they've lambed,' Beth told her. 'Some of them can't cope especially if they've had multiple births.

'We've got two lambs in a box by the Aga at the moment.' Beth looked at her watch, 'and either Mark or I must go very soon as they need feeding every four hours.'

'Night and day?'

'Yes, night and day.'

'We could help out if you like,' Kitty found herself saying as she poured herself another glass of wine.

'Kitty?' was Betty's only comment.

'If you and Mark told us what to do and we could call on you if there were problems, I'm sure we'd could help out. The kids will love it. What do you think Tom?'

'Lambs in a box by the Aga?' Tom reached out towards the jug of beer. 'Yes, why not. We wanted to be part of country life and I can't think of a better way to prove it. Bring 'em over Mark; we'll bottle feed them for you. It'll be a bit of fun won't it Kitty?'

Kitty nodded. It seemed that Tom wanted to share something with her. Something they could enjoy with the children and something that wasn't connected with that blasted car.

The next morning Mark delivered the two lambs that had been residing in Manor Farm's kitchen. Their place had already been taken by two more.

He showed Kitty how to feed them by holding the bottle so the lamb's head was up and the lamb was standing. On no account was she to cuddle them while feeding as the milk could get into their lungs and they could get pneumonia.

Sasha immediately named the lambs Dilly and Dally. They were to be kept warm and, to start with, fed 140ml from a bottle every four hours with a special formula.

Soon Dilly and especially the bolder, Dally, found they could scramble out of their box and followed Kitty round the kitchen; butting her legs for attention. They were shut in the old washhouse when she went out but at night they were back by the cosy warmth of the Aga.

The first night Kitty was so anxious about her new responsibilities that she slept on the kitchen Chesterfield but soon her maternal clock kicked in and she was awake and downstairs and ready with the bottles before the lambs began to bleat and baa.

Sasha, Midge and Xav all loved feeding the lambs and Tom managed one three o'clock feed but then he had to leave for some unscheduled meetings in the Seattle office.

When he had gone the days and especially the nights seemed long and lonely as sleep-deprived Kitty had to cope alone. She was longing for the weekend when Tom would be back to share the feeding and parenting of their own children as well as their woolly lodgers.

Kitty wasn't sure if it was the blackbird tuning up for the dawn chorus or the ping from her phone that woke her up.

Groping with bleary eyes she saw it was a text from Tom. Kitty nearly cried when she read that he had to prolong his trip as an extraordinary meeting had been called.

33

For Kitty this was the last straw especially as her brother-in-law and his sons had invited themselves over to see the lambs. Tristan and Dominic were not the easiest of children at the best of times but they tended to heed their uncle a lot more than their easy going father. This afternoon, poor Dilly and Dally would either be smothered with attention or tormented to bits.

Yawning, Kitty struggled out of bed as the first bleat of the day followed by a loud baa was heard from the kitchen.

**** **** ****

Chapter 7

The Aftermath

It was the sound of a car pulling into the yard that interrupted their concentration. During the sunny July afternoon Kitty and Rollo had been going through the papers and letters Rollo had sent and received following Tom's death.

'They can't be back already,' sighed Rollo putting documents containing details of Tom's pension into its folder. 'Your Mum and Dad said they'd keep the kids away until nearly bedtime.'

'It's Ted's car,' said Kitty looking through the open kitchen door. 'Wonder what he wants?'

'Is the ever gorgeous Simone with him or the malicious Melissa?'

'Don't think so but Chris is there and there's a flat-bed trailer attached to the car.'

By the time Rollo and Kitty were in the yard Ted Munroe had yanked open the workshop doors.

'Hello Ted, Chris,' called Rollo strolling over to where Chris was backing up the trailer. 'What a lovely surprise; coming in for a cuppa?'

'Hi Rollo, nice to see you. We didn't expect you'd still be here; did we Chris? Hello Kit, love. We won't come in as we're in a bit of a hurry and we've just come to pick up the car.'

'The car?'

'Yes, we reckoned you wouldn't want it hanging around as, y'know, a reminder.'

'As the police have said it isn't off limits anymore we thought we'd come over and take it away,' added Chris tossing aside a strip of the striped incident tape as he approached his sister-in-law. 'It's the best thing all round for all of us.'

Kitty stared in amazement. Since Tom had been discovered dead under the Jackson-Johnson she'd avoided thinking about it or looking at the workshop; leaving the strips of black and yellow tape sealing the double doors in place.

'I think we need to get this straight,' said Rollo. 'Speaking as Tom's executor, the car isn't yours to take. It is part of Tom's estate and, therefore, according to his Will, it belongs to Kitty. When and where it goes is entirely up to her.'

'I don't want the car,' Kitty was now on the verge of tears.

'So, we're doing you a favour in taking it off your hands. Come on Chris, back up a bit more.' Ted placed a brick against the workshop door to keep it open.

Kitty took a deep breath before speaking. 'I don't want the car but I haven't decided what I'm going to do with it. But I know what Tom paid for it and that it could be a valuable vehicle and although it caused his death and caused us to quarrel I am not yet ready to let it go.'

Ted Munroe put what he intended to be a caring fatherly arm round his daughter-in-law's shoulders. 'Kitty love; we understand. We only want to help you during this difficult time.' He paused as if to recall a phrase he'd been told to use. 'Letting the car go will help you to achieve closure.'

'I'm not ready to "achieve closure" as you call it and I've got Rollo to help me.'

'Rollo knows shit all about cars!' Chris laughed as he pushed the other door wide open. 'Kitty, let Dad and I get rid of it and we'll come to an … arrangement that suits all of us.'

'Arrangement?' Rollo's voice sounded cold and official. 'The Jackson-Johnson is Kitty's and when she "gets rid of it" she won't need "an arrangement". So, unless you want to reconsider the offer of tea I think you had better leave. Right Kitty?'

'Yes.' Kitty lifted her chin and made a real effort to keep her voice clear and calm. 'Goodbye Ted, Chris, I'll keep you informed about the car when I've decided what to do with it.'

Kitty clung on to Rollo's hand as they watched Chris manoeuvre out of the yard and drive away as fast as he dared considering the nature of the lane and the fact there was a rattling, empty trailer attached to the car to manoeuvre round Cowpat Corner.

Ted attempted a brief wave as they drove away, which Kitty didn't return. Before they'd entered the house Rollo was already on his phone.

The kettle hadn't reached boiling point before Mark was on his way up from Manor Farm with a heavy-duty padlock.

'Has Ted said anything about the car before?' Rollo asked as they drank their tea.

'No. Rollo, you know I don't want the bloody car. I wish it had never been bought or was festering away in someone else's fucking workshop.' Kitty paused to wipe away the angry tears, which were now pouring down her face. 'But I won't be taken advantage of by my father-in-law or my brother-in-law. It is a valuable car and that value belongs to me and to my children.'

Mark took a gulp of his tea; he had never seen Kitty so angry or so distraught before. Even after Tom's horrific accident she had been distressed and tearful but there hadn't been anger or even resentment about what had happened. But now, her in-laws' visit had seriously rattled her cage.

'I know a man in the car business,' he offered, 'and could get some advice if you like.'

'Thanks Mark,' said Rollo. 'Much appreciated. Now Kitty, has anything like this happened before?'

'Tell him Kitty,' Mark insisted.

'It wasn't about the car.'

'But it was an intrusion into your privacy and a trespass on to your property.'

Kitty sighed, 'I came home a week or so after the funeral and found Melissa in the scullery.'

'Why was she there and what was she doing?'

'She said she'd brought some smoked salmon for us and more of her blasted fruit salad as she was concerned that we might not be eating properly.'

'Cheeky cow,' was Rollo's only comment.

'Unfair on cows,' replied Mark. 'Tell him the rest Kitty.'

'Cupboard doors were open and so were some drawers. She said she'd been looking for a plate to put the food on although the salmon was still in the wrappers and the fruit salad in a plastic bowl.'

'How did she get in?'

'Through the kitchen door.'

'Kitty?'

'The door wasn't locked.'

'What!'

'It's the country - that's what you do.'

'Sorry Kitty, but that's an urban myth,' Mark laughed. 'Everything is locked, bolted and alarmed up to the hilt now. Maybe in my parents and grandparents' day that would've been true but not now. On Manor Farm we've CCTV everywhere and all the buildings and barns are as secure as Fort Knox.'

'And that's how it should be at Stoney Lea!' declared Rollo. 'Kitty, you lock up from now on and we'll get further security on the workshop. And leave spare keys with Mark and with Izzie. OK?'

Kitty nodded and gave him a reassuring smile as the sound of a car was heard in the yard.

It was her parents returning with the children.

Chapter 8

Rabbity Dreams

There was a little blue door Kitty had never seen before. She walked towards it over the newly mown grass and stretched out her hand towards the shiny doorknob. A prickly sensation filled her with a feeling of cold dread. Nevertheless she turned the knob and pushed open the door and stepped through.

There was the familiar long hallway and, as always there was a small brown rabbit dressed in a little blue coat with a large pocket watch in his hand. This was Kitty's old recurring dream - Peter Rabbit meets Alice in Wonderland. Sometimes she would find herself playing croquet with Mrs Tiggywinkle or being chased by the Mad Hatter with Benjamin Bunny pelting her with little, green apples from Mr McGregor's vegetable patch before she woke, hot and sweaty tangled up in the duvet, to the real world and the reality of the morning.

Kitty didn't know what caused the dream but she'd been having it on and off ever since Tom had died. Before that her dreams had been full of wild, crazy elements, which once she was awake faded away never to return. But now this rabbitty dream turned up at least once a week. Kitty believed if she could get to the bottom of whatever it was that triggered it she would be able to sort some of the tribulations, which filled her waking hours.

'Mummy, Mummy can we come in with you?'

Without waiting for an answer Sasha followed by Midge clambered in beside her. There was plenty of room as Tom's side was, as always, cold and empty.

'Mummy I don't want any more sleep but it's too dark to get up. So please tell me a story.'

'A story?'

'Yes. A story about a princess and a magic ...'

'Rabbit.'

'A magic rabbit Midge?'

'Yes. A magic rabbit that wants a...'

'An apple pie ... a magic apple pie.' Sasha was determined that Midge wasn't going to take control of the story.

39

This was a little too close to Kitty's recent dream for comfort.

'Come on Mummy, start. You know "once upon a time there was a ..."'

'A magic rabbit that was very shy and lonely as he had no friends ...'

'Did he have a mummy?'

'Yes Midge, he had a mummy.'

'Had his daddy died like our Daddy?'

Kitty just didn't know what the right answer was; did Midge want everyone to be fatherless just like himself and his sister?

'His daddy has gone a long way away to work and is busy and happy,' said Sasha. 'Get on with the story Mummy. Get to the bit with the princess.'

'Well, the rabbit decided he would go on an adventure so he could find himself some friends ...'

As the story rolled on to its "happy ever after" conclusion the three of them snuggling into a tightly knot of entwined arms and legs under the duvet until they all drifted off into dreamless sleep which was rudely disturbed by the simultaneous ringing of Kitty's mobile phone and a loud hammering on the kitchen door.

Dreams about rabbits had disturbed Kitty's night and stories about rabbits had caused them to oversleep and now Sasha would be late for school.

Chapter 9

October

Kitty put the phone down, the banality of her own words still echoing in her head. The daily reassurances she gave her mother, father and friends far and near had at first worked. It was as if her subconscious had begun to believe all the half-truths. But now they meant nothing and the same numbness she'd felt five months ago when the news of Tom's accident had been broken to her returned at increasingly frequent intervals.

Sometimes she felt she was drowning in the grey depths of ineffectual lethargy. The previous day she'd taken Midge to the village playgroup in his pyjamas. Mrs Dale hadn't said a word as she'd ushered Midge to join the others in the welcome circle but he had been wearing a pair of shorts and one of the playgroup's brilliant blue t-shirts when she'd collected him. His Spiderman pyjamas came home neatly folded in a carrier bag.

Today Kitty was positive that there was something important she had to do. But as she couldn't think what it was or be bothered to check the kitchen notice board she sat down on the old Chesterfield, close to the comforting warmth of the Aga and started to read last week's paper. Apparently a minor royal had visited the local hospital and a secondary school before taking tea with a pair of centenarian twins who attributed their long life to whist, gardening and hot milk and gin at bedtime.

Kitty associated whist with wet Welsh childhood holidays and although the idea of a gin was tempting; hot milk was not. So she went out into the garden.

Outside the lawn was still covered with dew and spiders' webs. Purple Michaelmas daisies filled the borders clashing with the brilliant shocking cerise of the nirenes.

The fact that the garden looked neat and tidy was a continual surprise. Under Mrs Finchcock's directive Mr Finchcock turned up once a week to mow the lawns, keep the weeds under control and the kitchen garden productive.

Wandering through the brick arch Kitty viewed the neatness of that same kitchen garden. It looked so reassuring with the rectangular beds lined with orderly rows of leeks, potatoes, sprouts and cabbages. In a sunny corner were Sasha and Midge's sunflowers. The huge, drooping heads now brown were full of fat black seeds. Next to them the delicate flowers on the Jerusalem artichokes looked like poor relations.

Tom had been amused but incredulous when Rollo had turned up on the first of his frequent visits with a case of champagne "to see us through the weekend", a sheep-shaped doormat, brightly coloured welly boots for the children, bubble bath for Kitty and a large book on growing vegetables for beginners.

As there were two walled gardens at Stoney Lea along with fruit cages, an orchard of assorted trees, two greenhouses and a lean-to which Mrs Redman had called the bothy it looked as if Rollo's book would become a well-thumbed necessity.

Outside the never used front door there was a large lawn and flowerbeds, a lily pond complete with goldfish and a pergola which, in the summer was covered by creamy white rambling roses.

The first year they had all managed, through trial and error, to produce a reasonable harvest. The freezer had been filled with: French and runner beans, gooseberries, rhubarb, apple slices, plums and greengages. The larder shelves had gleaming rows of: blackcurrant, raspberry and strawberry jam as well as spicy apple, plum and green tomato chutney.

This year the sweetcorn had grown well and was now almost as tall as the sunflowers. 'The corn is as high as an elephant's eye' sang Kitty's brain. Where had she heard it before? It sounded familiar but was somehow totally original. That had been happening quite a lot since Tom's accident. A tune would, uninvited, enter her head and take over. Rollo had said it was 'an earworm' which had worried Sasha who was going through an intense interest in everything that crept and crawled.

'You should dry roast those sunflower seeds in the bottom oven of the Aga or you could just leave them for the goldfinches. They love sunflower seeds.'

Kitty turned to see Mrs Finchcock coming through the arch.

'Finchcock has done a good job here. You'll have a better crop of leeks than we'll have at Reeve House. We're too near the Eden for successful yields. '

'Hello Mrs Finchcock, how lovely to see you,' Kitty tucked her sodden hankie away and tried out a smile. 'Would you like a cup of coffee?' Kitty was aware that the social niceties had come out in a breathless rush and so now she was stuck with what to say or do next.

'Thank you Kitty, but we've no time for coffee. I need you to come with me to collect the new set of crockery for the village hall. We'll need it for Sunday's Harvest Supper.'

Kitty was at a loss of what to say or think. Eventually she came up with; 'But there's Midge. Playgroup finishes at ...'

'That's all taken care of. I saw Goat Shed Izzie and she is going to pick Midge up and she'll give him some lunch as well.'

'But ...'

'No buts - it is all arranged'.

'I'll get my coat.'

'Kitty dear, you need more than your coat; you're still in your dressing gown and pyjamas. Pop upstairs and get yourself washed and dressed and then we'll be off.'

When she came downstairs Kitty found that Mrs Finchcock had washed the children's breakfast dishes and coffee mugs and was just finishing sweeping the kitchen floor.

'You'll be infested with mice if you allow the floor to get into this state. This is the countryside my dear, the whole place is alive with vermin and the little blighters will be in the house nibbling away at everything given half a chance. What you need is a cat.'

'A cat?'

'Yes, the Redmans always had a couple of moggies. Good mousers the pair of them. What you need is a yard cat. I'll look out for a couple of kittens. There's always someone in the village with kittens that need a home.'

'I'm not sure about cats; Midge had chest problems when he was a baby. We thought he might develop asthma.'

'Has he had any problems since you moved here?'

'No, but ...'

'He's most likely grown out of it but I'll make sure they are shorthaired kittens all the same. Don't let Sasha spoil them, as you need them to work.

'Now, are you ready? Good, we'd better be off although with a bit of luck it won't take us long to get to Stoke.'

The journey was uneventful. Mrs Finchcock didn't chat and the restful sounds of Classic FM induced in Kitty a stillness, which soothed and focussed her thoughts.

Under Rollo's strict instructions she had finally gone through her incoming and outgoings ready for his next visit. Tom had dealt with everything; the mortgage, utilities and household bills, the whole lot. Even to her inexperienced eye she could see that she'd have to become more businesslike even though Rollo had promised to take care of it all.

From the start Rollo had assured her that Tom's life insurance would pay up and therefore there would be no trouble with the mortgage and he'd made sure all the forms she'd had to fill in were sent to the right place at the right time.

The big decision had been whether or not to stay at Stoney Lea. To move back to where they'd lived before and been so happy was one option. But if they hadn't moved Tom would most likely still be alive.

Although she loved her parents dearly, George and Betty had their own lives to live. The distance from Stoney Lea wasn't too far to easily visit them or for them to pop over. Living closer to Ted and Simone Munroe was not an alternative she even started to contemplate.

So, Kitty decided that, for the time being, they would stay at Stoney Lea. Sasha and Midge seemed happy and, in a strange way she was too. She'd made good friends in the village and had wonderful support from a lot of people like Mrs Finchcock and Mrs Selby, the forceful lady who ran the village shop and post office.

When she was thinking clearly she still wanted to achieve all the alterations that they had planned. Bathrooms were the first priority. An upstairs loo was more than essential because the downstairs bathroom was just that bit too far for Midge's nocturnal trips. It was no use fitting stair carpets until that problem had been resolved.

Kitty felt a surge of familiar anger. If only bloody Tom hadn't spent the money earmarked for the bathrooms on that bloody car Midge wouldn't be found crying in the middle of the night in a puddle on the stairs and Tom would still be here.

With Sasha, Midge and Xavier busily sticking sparkly bits on to paper crowns; Kitty, sitting on the patchwork-covered sofa, sipped a mug of strong tea by the Goat Shed's wood burning stove as outside the late October afternoon light began to fade.

'I love that painting,' Kitty remarked gesturing with her mug to a large oil painting. 'It's the light coming through the clouds and the way it blends into the landscape. You can almost feel the wind and hear the skylarks.'

'It's of Hatherstone Hills. My great aunt painted it. She was evacuated to the village during the war and returned to stay with the family as often as she could.' Izzie paused. 'It inspired me to come and live here and it was her legacy that enabled me to buy this cottage.'

Kitty was startled; Izzie was very sparing in disclosing any information about her life so, rather than making further enquiries she sipped her tea.

While Izzie was often pointed out as the village's arty weirdo as she had a talent for turning her hand to a variety of handiwork skills and turning out bright, garments for herself and her son and preferring to cycle round the village on an old sit-up-and-beg bicycle; keeping her precious VW Beetle for essential trips.

But since Tom's accident Kitty had come to appreciate Izzie's kindness and understanding. She had never told Kitty to "pull herself together" or to "move on". She had handed her boxes of tissues, cups of tea, the occasional G&T, listened to her maudlin rambles, minded and fed Sasha and Midge on numerous occasions and gently persuaded Kitty to tackle some of the chaos that at times seemed to overwhelm her.

Now Izzie, stitching bright red crocheted poppies on to the brim of a conker-brown felt hat, was giving her friend time to reflect and relax.

'I wasn't really needed at the pottery,' Kitty told her. 'Everything was ready and we didn't even have to lift the boxes into the car.'

Izzie said nothing.

'The factory shop was interesting. I bought a lovely big plate for my mother's birthday and some new mugs for us.'

Izzie threaded a long piece of scarlet silk through her needle'

'Mrs Finchcock was quite chatty when we were in the cafe; much more human and approachable than she seems in the village. She was telling me what it was like when they first came to the village and how the locals regarded them as intruders.' Kitty paused. 'I expect the whole thing was one of Mrs Finchcock's stratagems to involve me in village life and get me out the house.'

'But you are involved in village life.' Izzie commented. 'You supported the village fête and the school sports day.'

'That was because of the children.'

'I won the egg and spoon,' Sasha placed her crown on her mother's head before draping herself across her lap. 'Mrs Drummond has asked everyone to bring a con-trib-u-shun to decorate the church for the Harvest Festival. Afterwards it'll all go to the hospital and to the poor and lonely. I told her we'd bring some potatoes and cabbages as we've got lots.' Sasha sat up and curled her fingers into Kitty's hair. 'Mrs Drummond said I was to ask you if we were going to the Harvest Supper as if we are we have to sign up.'

'Oh Sasha, I don't know. Midge is too little to stay up so late and ... I'm just not sure ...'

'Please Mummy, everyone is going and Alice says there are games and lots and lots to eat.'

'I'll go if you'll go,' offered Izzie.

Kitty was surprised. Izzie usually had nothing to do with any church related activities.

'Xavier mentioned it yesterday and Midge will be fine as its half term next week so everyone can sleep in on Monday. Do you think I should make some ears of wheat to go with the poppies? They would be appropriate for the festivities.'

'Well ...'

'That's settled then. How about if I come over on Saturday afternoon and we can have a massive baking session as our contribution to this post-pagan feast to supplement the cabbages? Now, who would like to help me cook some pancakes for tea?'

As the children, paper crowns on their heads, rushed to help Izzie in her tiny kitchen Kitty felt that for the second time that day she had been manipulated, but somehow, once again, it felt right.

Chapter 10

Giving it a Go

'Give it a go,' her friends told her. 'It'll do you good', they'd assured her'. It'll be a laugh', they'd promised and for their final argument; 'an excuse to get your glad rags out of mothballs'.

'Glad rags': the phrase was not just antiquated but to Kitty totally inappropriate. What do I have to be glad about; she thought as she gazed at the assortment of clothes she'd crammed anyhow to fill the space in the big wardrobe unable to bear the emptiness where Tom's suits had once hung.

Rollo has insisted that they packed up Tom's clothes the last time he'd been up. It had been a task she'd been dreading and, therefore, avoiding. So, Rollo arranged for Sasha and Midge to spend the day with Izzie and Xavier and had poured them both huge brandies before they'd started on the terrible task.

'Where will you take them?' Kitty had asked as she folded jackets after Rollo had checked the pockets.

'There's plenty who will get good use out of them. Have you any preferences?'

'I haven't really given it a thought. It's not something you plan to do; defrost the fridge, buy washing powder and give your dead husband's clothes away.'

'I've a mate who is a prison visitor. He told me that suits are useful for cons when they go for placement interviews before their release or there are homeless refuges or charity shops?'

'Any or all of them will do, I'll leave it up to you.' Kitty shook out a shirt. 'Rollo, please get rid of everything somewhere a long way from here. I don't want to see one of Tom's jackets on a stranger when I'm in Ashbourne market. At this stage, I don't even care if you burn them'

Rollo gave her a comforting squeeze before folding Tom's favourite jacket and placing it with infinite care into another of the large striped bags.

Kitty had insisted that as Tom's clothes had to go they would go in style and not crammed into black bin bags. So she had gone to the market and bought twenty of the heavy-duty striped bags, which were usually used to take washing to the laundrette.

Rollo had asked to keep a couple of Tom's ties and Kitty kept the chunky grey jersey they'd bought in the Hebrides on their honeymoon, in fact if she wasn't wearing it she often discovered the children curled up on the kitchen Chesterfield cuddled up inside it, each with an arm down one of the sleeves.

But tonight she was going on the town with Beth and Goat Shed Izzie but none of her clothes seemed suitable.

Beth had talked about wearing red but red wasn't one of Kitty's colours and Izzie was one of the most bizarrely dressed persons she'd ever met so she could be wearing red, purple, sky blue or a combination of all three with lace accessories and still look sensational. Beth would look chic wearing a chicken feed sack.

Eventually Izzie had advised her to wearing something she'd be comfortable moving around in. For Pilates and the legs, bums and tums classes Kitty had tried after Midge had been born she'd worn leggings and a baggy t-shirt over her leotard but for her first tango lesson in the town hall's function room she didn't think lycra would be appropriate.

The image of herself in fishnets and a tight, shiny black skirt slashed to the thigh flashed through her mind. This was followed by the vision of herself with a crimson rose between her teeth and a sexy, smouldering *señor* spinning her round and round on a moonlit Argentinian piazza.

There were no fishnets or split skirts in the heap of garments on her bed but by the time Beth's car turned up in the yard she hoped she was more or less suitably dressed.

'That wasn't too bad was it?' Izzie asked her two friends as they left the town hall.

'Better than a trip to the dentists and not as bad as paying bills,' admitted Beth reaching in her bag for her car keys. 'What about you Kitty?'

Hot tango rhythms still filled Kitty's head. The ordeal had turned out better than she expected. She felt that she'd had the first real fun in months and strangely enough, she didn't feel guilty.

'There's something I'd like to say about this evening. First, we now know the correct dress code for tango lessons in Uttoxeter and secondly, if we're going to carry on with these classes we're going to have to get a lot fitter and fast.'

Beth gave Izzie what her mother would call an old-fashioned look. She hadn't expected tango dancing as therapy to have such an immediate and positive effect.

The next morning Kitty ached in places she hadn't previously known existed but, nevertheless, she found herself trying out a few of the steps as she prepared breakfast and made up Sasha's packed lunch.

With her newly acquired realism she was aware that this light heartedness might not last but at the moment she really felt like dancing.

Sweeping Midge up and grabbing hold of Sasha's hand she danced all around the kitchen until Sasha pointed out they would be late for school.

Chapter 11

November

'What are you going to do about Christmas?'

Kitty had dreaded being directly asked although the question had been going round and round her head for weeks like the whirring of a child's plastic windmill.

'Oh Sue, I don't know.' Kitty paused and walked over to look out of the kitchen window. Outside the puddles in the yard were still frozen and the gate rimed with overnight frost although the sky was a bright, clear blue.

'Kitty? Are you still there? You could all come to us. I can arrange it that it'll just be Mike and me and the kids. Think about it Kitty.'

Kitty thought of the organised clutter of Sue and Mike's house once as familiar as her own. She could, and at times had, managed Sue's kitchen as easily and as efficiently as she had run her own. But she knew to return to where she and Tom had spent so many happy get-togethers would, at present, be wrong.

'That wouldn't be fair on your parents or on Lottie and Luke as they wouldn't be seeing their grandparents.'

'Mum and Dad will understand.'

'It's very kind of you but no thank you.'

'You're sure?'

Kitty knew that her oldest friend wanted to do everything she could to help and support her. 'Yes, I'm sure.'

'So, what will you do? What are your parents doing?'

'It's a bit awkward. Dad is taking Mum away on a Caribbean cruise as their fortieth anniversary is just before Christmas. Mum says she'll miss being with the children and having a traditional Christmas but Dad has turned all romantic and wants to sip martinis on the sun deck and dance the night away under a tropical moon.'

'Your dad; drinking cocktails?' Sue laughed. 'I've always thought of him as a real ale connoisseur.'

'He is but I think it is part of his strategy of pretending things are normal and this is what he'd promised Mum.' Kitty paused. 'Maybe he's right and if we all pretend what is happening is normal then it will be. What was normal last year will never be … normal again.'

'Oh Kitty!'

Even over the telephone Kitty knew Sue was crying.

Christmas had been on Kitty's mind ever since half-term when Rollo had asked her what she was planning to do.

Feeling courageous after the success of the Harvest Supper and the warm welcome she and the children had received from the village community she'd told him that she didn't think Christmas would be a problem. She wanted to be at home at Stoney Lea with the children and of course, there were the hens and now, there was the definite prospect of kittens to consider. And Rollo, as always, would be there to support her.

Looking back, last year's Christmas had been such a happy time as they had filled Stoney Lea with family and friends. The house had been warm not only from log fires burning in the dining and sitting rooms, and the Aga keeping the kitchen warm and snug and of course, now the central heating and new boiler had been installed everywhere, except for the downstairs bathroom, felt gloriously warm and cosy.

It had been easy to make the old stone farmhouse look festive. Together they had all gone in the lanes and woods and gathered armfuls of evergreens and crammed great boughs of well-berried holly behind the pictures and mirrors in the dining room and sitting room while fairy lights twinkled through garlands of ivy and old man's beard which they'd twined along the kitchen beams. Mark had contributed a huge bunch of mistletoe cut from an ancient oak tree in one of the woods on Manor Farm.

Kitty had been in despair of getting spilt glitter from between the grain of the kitchen table. Decorating homemade Christmas cards had kept Sasha and Midge quiet for hours as had sticking strips of brightly, coloured paper into paper-chains, which Tom had strung over the doorways.

The crowning glory had been the Christmas tree. Tom's argument that a Range Rover was an essential part of country living became a reality as he managed to transport the biggest tree he could find with ease.

The tree placed by the kitchen window festooned with white fairy lights and shiny red, gold and silver baubles. When lit, it's light streamed across the yard, shining like a welcoming beacon of light and love, all through that frosty, festive season.

51

Christmas Day had been wonderful and in Kitty's mind a triumph. She was now quite at home with the Aga and cooking for the extended family of her parents, all Tom's family and, of course, Rollo hadn't been a problem although she was pleased that her mum and dad and Rollo were there to peel vegetables, clear away and load and empty the dishwasher. True to form Tom's family did nothing apart from open more bottles and occasionally put a log on one or other of the fires.

Before and after Christmas they had joyfully joined in with all the village festivities - manning the mince pies and mulled wine stall at the Christmas Market and carol singing on frosty evenings around the parish. Midge, dressed up as a sheep, and Sasha, as an angel, took part in the church's crib service. There had been invitations to children's parties, Christmas drinks, and a tea party after the village pantomime. Although Sasha and Midge were reluctant to take down the decorations and discard the tree by the time Twelfth Night had come around Kitty was relieved that the new school term had started and normality returned.

This year, Kitty decided, she would make sure Christmas was still a special occasion, for the children's sake as well as her own. Rollo would support her and she'd invite Izzie and Xav to join them as well as extending an invitation to all her in-laws There'd be lights, a Christmas tree and all the rest of the traditional fare and if her eyes were red from crying and if she clung to the children more than usual she was sure no one would object.

After assuring Sue that everything would be fine Kitty picked up one of Sasha's glittery pens and a piece of paper and wrote on the top My Christmas To Do List before bursting into tears.

Chapter 12

Kittens

Kitty knelt down on the rug in Mrs Selby's kitchen and picked up a wriggling black kitten.

Sasha, lying on her tummy, shook a bunch of pink and purple feathers tied to a piece of green ribbon towards the boldest member of the litter who put out a tentative paw to trap it.

For once Mrs Finchcock and Mrs Selby were in agreement. Although both ladies usually kept up a high degree of frosty reserve as they both considered themselves to be *the* village leader, on this December afternoon they seemed to have agreed on an amiable truce.

As sub post mistress and village shopkeeper, Mrs Selby was able to keep an eye on both the elderly and the younger members of the village as they frequented the village shop for provisions, pensions, banking facilities, sweets and chat and therefore was often the first to hear and consequently the first one to spread 'news'.

As a school governor, a member of the Parish Council, senior church flower arranger and chairperson of the WI Mrs Finchcock felt she had her finger on the pulse of the village; and although, not in actual fact a gossip, she had the authority to keep a look out for the villagers and determine how events were organised.

Today though, they were in perfect accord - two of the kittens would be perfect for Kitty, Sasha and Midge.

'They won't be ready to leave their mother for another two weeks,' Mrs Selby told Sasha who was eager to take them home straight away. 'But you can choose which ones you'd like and come and see them at any time.'

'A dangerous promise,' laughed Kitty picking up another kitten. 'You'll have Sasha camping on your doorstep.

'Look Midge, this one has a sweet little white star on its chest. Would you like this one?'

'They are all girls,' grumbled Midge stroking the soft black fur. 'Why can't we have two boys or a boy and a girl?'

53

'Freda has only had girl kittens in this litter,' Mrs Selby told him stroking the kitten's mother who was warily watching the unfamiliar humans handling her kittens. 'She usually has a mixed lot.'

'Look how sweet and playful they are,' pointed out Kitty as by now Sasha had all four kittens attacking the feathery toy.

'Would you rather wait for some other kittens?' asked Mrs Finchcock.

'No!' Sasha was adamant. 'We want the kittens to be with us for Christmas. Isn't that right, Mummy?'

'It would be nice.'

'So, Midge you have that one,' Sasha pointed to the one with the star on its chest, 'and I'll have this one.' and she picked up the bold kitten who by now was surrounded by pink and purple feathers.

'Good,' said Mrs Finchcock. 'You'll have time to get everything ready for them.'

'You must make sure they have a warm, snug place to sleep and that they don't get out when you open the kitchen door,' advised Mrs Selby.

'We'll make signs for inside and outside the door and the windows will stay closed,' Sasha promised.

'You must be very quiet and gentle with them until they settle down and really know you. Have you thought what to call them?'

'Sooty and Sweep would be appropriate,' Mrs Finchcock began to put on her coat.

'Maybe we should wait to see what suits their personalities,' Kitty rescued a kitten and put it back in the box with its mother. 'But as they will be with us for Christmas we could think up Christmassy names.'

'An excellent idea,' declared Mrs Finchcock who was now ready to leave. 'What about Holly and Ivy?'

'This one is Ivy,' decided Sasha as she put the bold kitten back in the box. 'And this is Holly,' she pointed to the one with the white star.

'Both girls' names,' grumbled Midge.

'You could give her a nickname,' suggested Mrs Selby. 'Buddy goes with Holly so you could call her Buddy. That's a boy's name.'

'Goodbye Buddy,' whispered Sasha to the newly named kitten. 'We'll call you Buddy but remember your real name is Holly.'

' "All my love, all my kisses," ' sang Mrs Finchcock as she walked back to her car, "You don't know what you're missin' ..." '

'Oh boy!' thought Kitty trying to smother a giggle. She realised that to name a kitten after a 1950s pop star was meaningless to the children. But once Kitty got the giggles that was it. Her mind glided effortlessly into remembering an old magazine she had flicked through at the dentists. It was a soppy story about a cat that needed a blood transfusion and the headline trumpeted "Holly and the IV."

Chapter 13

Bother in the Bothy

Things were vanishing. On Monday morning Kitty wasted a lot of time looking for Midge's swimming towel and the tartan picnic rug had disappeared as well. Tom's navy waxed Barbour was the next thing to go missing.

Kitty knew she'd left it hanging on the back of the scullery door after the children came home from school. But when she went to wear it to lock up the hens it wasn't there.

For weeks after Tom's death there had been a period when she was continually mislaying things. At times this hadn't bothered her and she had either carried on without the necessary scissors or Sellotape or just left the task unfinished. Hence Lottie's birthday present was only delivered safe and sound because Mrs Selby, in the Post Office, re-wrapped, taped and re-addressed it for her.

Eventually wayward items would turn up tucked in among the tea towels or in the fridge or, in the case of the Sellotape, nestling among the flakes in a cereal packet. But now Kitty felt that she was well over that unsettling phase. She distinctly remembered taking the rug out of the car after the village May Day festivities and putting it away and she knew she'd washed Midge's swimming towel at the weekend and she was sure she had hung up the jacket on the back of the door earlier that day.

Other things also alerted her that something was up; Sasha and Midge were helping themselves to biscuits and fruit without asking and on the last two mornings there had been no bread in the bread crock when she'd been convinced there was enough left overnight for breakfast.

During coffee with Izzie and Beth, thinly disguised as a planning meeting about the school's cake stall, Kitty decided that enough was enough and she needed guidance.

'Have any of your kids ever become sneaky thieves?'

'Things going missing?' Izzie raised an eyebrow.

'Mm,' answered Kitty.

'Is it money or just things?'

'Just things - as far as I can see. I know I had that spell of losing stuff a while ago but this is different. It's the picnic rug and Midge's swimming towel and the jar of Marmite and apples and bread. Do you think its subliminal behaviour because of Tom?'

'I doubt it,' said Izzie. 'I think it would've happened sooner if it was that. Do you suspect Sasha or Midge or both of them?'

'Both of them but Midge could be going along with Sasha.'

'Just the rug and the towel?' Izzie asked.

'Maybe they are making a den,' suggested Beth ticking bunting off a list.

'I thought of that but Tom's waxed Barbour went missing yesterday and I know I left it hanging behind the scullery door.'

'Any other odd behaviour?'

'Well, they're both asking for more snacks or just helping themselves as well as eating me out of house and home. There's been an absolute rush on peanut butter and Sasha doesn't really like it.'

'Have you looked in their rooms or been through their pockets?'

'Yes but there was nothing there apart from a couple of sticky plates from the doll's tea set under Sasha's bed which might have had jam on them and a couple of teaspoons and a fruit knife in one of Midge's wellies.'

'Have you asked them about them?'

'Mm – not really although I did talk to them about not keeping secrets about important things.'

'Xav hasn't mentioned anything unusual happening as school. Anything out of the ordinary going on at home?'

'We were all disappointed that Rollo couldn't come up at the weekend. We were going to reinforce the chicken run as something was trying to dig its way in.'

'I'll ask Mark to send Geoff to sort it out,' offered Beth refilling their mugs.

'Thanks but there's no need; Mr Finchcock fixed it yesterday.'

'Mr Finchcock?'

'Yes, he usually comes up on Tuesdays.'

'But the Finchcocks were at the Chelsea Flower Show. They went down on Sunday to stay with one of their sons.'

'You're sure?'

'Yes, Mrs Selby saw them on TV last night amongst the crowds looking at a show garden. Mrs Finchcock was wearing her green jacket.'

'But the enclosure has been fixed and there was a basket of spring greens and a couple of trimmed lettuce by the back door.'

'Does Mr Finchcock usually pick veg for you?'

'Sometimes. He's kind of reminding me of what's ready.'

Izzie reached for her bag, 'I'll come back with you and we'll have a look around.'

'There's no need Izzie. Most likely someone just dropped them round as a ... gift.'

'And the chicken run; was the job done well?'

'Yes.'

Beth and Izzie looked at each other.

'We'll both come with you. I'd get Mark but he and Geoff have taken a lorry load of bullocks to the livestock auction in Leek.'

Nothing looked out of place in Stoney Lea's front yard, Midge's red bike was lying by the workshop door, which was still bolted and triple padlocked and Sasha's skipping rope was where she'd left it the night before; looped over the gate to the front garden.

The kitchen door was locked, as was the scullery door. However, the gate into the small yard from the kitchen garden was ajar and Kitty knew it'd been closed when she'd pegged out some washing that morning.

As Izzie pushed open the gate Beth had her thumb hovering over the 9 on her mobile - just in case an emergency call was necessary.

Kitty looked around the individual vegetable beds noting the spindly sticks for the delicate pea plants and the more robust tepees for the runner beans and where Mr Finchcock had planted out the young cauliflower and cabbage seedlings ensuring they would have vegetables to last them throughout the year. She knew without his help she would never have been able to keep up the garden.

There was a gap in a row of young lettuces where some had been lifted. 'You said there was lettuce by the back door? One or two?' Izzie asked.

'Two but that space would've been for at least three.'

Beth pointed to a garden tap filling a large watering can and to someone kneeling among the rows of broad beans. 'I don't think that's Mr McGregor,' she whispered.

'Or Peter Rabbit.' Izzie raised her voice, 'Good morning. May we help you?'

The man crouched between the beans stood up and walked over to switch off the garden tap before turning to face them. Kitty was relieved to see that he didn't look menacing or particularly dangerous He was perhaps in his mid-

58

forties, quite tall and wearing faded jeans tucked into, what Kitty was sure were Tom's wellingtons. His arms and face were tanned although he needed a shave. As he walked towards them he ran his fingers through his unruly, brown hair as if to appear a little more presentable.

'Good morning - I think I owe the lady of the house,' and here he inclined his head towards Kitty, 'an explanation and an apology.'

Not knowing quite what to say Kitty surprised herself by inviting him in for a cup of tea.

Izzie and Beth sat cradling their mugs while watching the man devour the plate of eggs, bacon and fried bread Kitty had quickly cooked for him. Beth's phone was on the table and Izzie knew that for two pins she'd ring the police.

'Thank you, that was very welcome,' said the man placing his knife and fork together. 'Now, I expect you'd like to have an explanation of why I was dossing down in the bothy and why Sasha and Midge have been supplying me with sandwiches?'

He shyly smiled at his would be interrogators. 'I can assure you I'm not a creep or a paedophile and it is not a reboot of *Whistle down the Wind*.'

All three women took a sip of their tea as in agreement. They already knew his name was Joe Saxon and that he had been sleeping in the bothy since Sunday.

'Believe me, I haven't done nothing wrong and I'm not wanted by the police, the army or any official body.' Here he gave a nod towards Beth's phone. 'The only wrong I have done is towards myself … and to what is left of my family.' He lifted his mug as if to take a drink but put it back on the table and stared into its milky depths.

'Take your time,' said Izzie putting a hand on his arm. 'The truth can be hard but we want the truth or we will ring the police.'

Joe gave her a weak smile and began.

'I'm a carpenter and furniture maker by trade and live … lived in Applethwaite in Cumbria. I worked alongside my father and we had a good little business.'

'Had?' queried Izzie.

'Aye, had,' Joe drank some of his tea. 'It all went tits up after my father and … my wife were both killed in a car accident,' he paused.

'When was this?' asked Kitty.

'Four years ago last Christmas.'

'Four years ago? Wasn't that when there were those awful floods in Carlisle?

'Aye, and not only in Carlisle,' Joe gave a bitter laugh. 'And it wasn't the first time either. We'd been flooded before but we'd managed to get through it and survived but this time it was different.'

Kitty remembered seeing the disaster on the news and in the papers; furniture, toys and Christmas trees still decked with baubles and fairy lights floating out of flooded houses and into the streets and people wading waist deep in water clutching possessions, cats, dogs and their children and old folk being rowed away from their flooded homes.

'Have you any other family?'

'There's Frannie, my daughter. At first we tried to comfort each other but we were wrapped in our own separate grief. She'd lost her mum and her granddad and I'd lost my Mary. We'd been sweethearts since we were children.'

'Joseph and Mary … just like?' whispered Beth.

'Aye and cast together in the school Nativity play when we were little 'uns and together for the next twenty one years.'

The only sound in the kitchen at that moment was the persistent, gentle tick of the clock.

'You said this was?' asked Izzie putting a fresh mug of coffee in front of him.

'Four years ago, four years of absolute hell when it seemed that it didn't stop raining,' Joe laughed in a derisory way. 'On the day of the funeral the Beck burst its banks and the village was flooded.

'We were flooded out – the house, the workshop everything. I suppose there was a sense of everyone helping each other but I wasn't really aware of it.' Joe picked up his mug but put it down without drinking.

'Folk were wonderful and I tried to carry on at first for Frannie's sake but the house was a mess and the workshop even worse with wood warped, tools and finished pieces ruined. I tried but not hard enough and when the place flooded again last back end ...

'I suppose I had a kind of breakdown and truth be known I had been on the lash more than working. The business was ruined and what work I had in progress was washed away and there was nothing left to make me want to start again,'

'But you were insured?' asked Beth as she gathered up her phone and keys. It was nearly time to pick up Harry and Midge from the playgroup.

'There wasn't any insurance. Like hundreds of others after the first flood the insurance companies left us stranded. Some policies were declared invalid by some obscure clause buried deep in the small print or in my case they insisted that the storm was not to blame for the floods and so refused to pay my so-called Act of God, 'weather-related' claim.

'That's disgraceful!' Beth was as horrified. She was married to a man who read and re-read all the small print from instructions to assembling the children's play-tent to the handbook accompanying his new skid steer loader.

'What about your daughter … Frannie? How did she take all this?' Kitty knew she wouldn't have survived the last year without the support of her family and friends and the fact that Sasha and Midge needed her.

'When her mum was … killed,' Joe paused and bit his bottom lip before continuing. 'Fran was … stunned. She was in her second year of a nursing degree at Ligbury Uni and she wanted to drop out and stay home to help me … to help each other. But I insisted she stayed on. She came home quite regularly at first but then we kind of drifted and I haven't seen her for over a year. I think she might still in the Ligbury area.'

'What happened?' insisted Izzie.

'I … went to pieces. There's no other explanation. I'd lost Mary and after that the house and the business meant nothing so I took to drink. I'd never been a real drinking man; maybe the odd pint now and then or a glass of wine with me dinner or on special occasions but now, my best friends became *Johnny Walker, Jack Daniels and Captain Morgan.*'

Beth opened the door, mouthing as she left to Izzie and Kitty to let her know what happened.

'We need to have this settled before Midge and Harry arrive,' said Kitty.

'Midge is a great little lad,' Joe gave Kitty a small smile. 'He and Sasha saved me bacon.'

'Joe,' ordered Izzie, 'get on with it.'

'Well, there was no work and I owed some customers as they'd paid a deposit for bespoke pieces. But I hadn't the materials, tools or inclination to finish them. In the end I gave up and when, last back end, the place flooded again … well, that was it and I just walked.'

'What do you mean "walked"?'

'It was 21st December, the anniversary of Mary's death and I walked away from the whole damn lot; what was left of the workshop, the house, my life, everything.'

'Did you know where you were going?'

'Nope.'

Kitty was now beginning to feel afraid. What if she had invited a madman into her kitchen? What if that same madman had harmed her children? She wished Beth had left her mobile phone or that her own wasn't in her jacket pocket.

Izzie must've sensed Kitty's concern so she put her own mobile on to the table. 'What was your plan?'

'I didn't have one. I felt a tad guilty at leaving but I knew I had to get away from Applethwaite and all the memories. So, I packed up me van and drove south. I managed all right for a while. I slept in the van and found some casual work on farms and veg lifting. But me van got nicked just outside Macclesfield.'

'Macclesfield?'

'Yeah. I lost everything again apart what was in me pockets and the bread, milk, ham and the couple of loo rolls I'd just bought in an old carrier bag.'

'Did the police trace your van?'

'Nah and to tell the truth they weren't really bothered.'

'So, what did you do?' Kitty asked.

'Got drunk?' guessed Izzie.

'Right first time and somehow or other I overheard someone talking about an archaeological dig in the Hatherstone Hills and I remembered me Dad had an aunt who lived near there and so I thought I'd visit her.'

'You decided to visit your great-aunt? If she's still alive how old would she be?'

'Dunno but it seemed a good idea at the time so I set off – walking.'

'When was this?' asked Kitty.

'Last Friday … I think. I remember sleeping by a lake and scrounging some breakfast in Leek and starting off towards Ashbourne but after that it's a bit hazy.'

'How did you end up here?'

'I'm not really sure. At one point I know a lorry driver gave me a lift.'

'And how did my children find you?'

'I'd had a couple of tumbles and to tell the truth I was feeling a bit light headed. I sat by a bit of a wall and noticed it needed patching up a bit. I've not done much dry stonewalling but I decided to have a go and when I turned round there were these kids watching me. Sasha looked so like Frannie when she was a little 'un that it all got too much for me and I started to cry and at the same time it started to rain.

'So they brought me to the bothy and fetched me a towel and some biscuits and apples and later on a rug and some jam and peanut butter sandwiches. I'm not a peanut butter fan but they did taste good.'

'You didn't question them or ask to speak to their parents?' Izzie enquired.

'I was so weary and that tired that I didn't think. I slept through and the next morning there were more sandwiches, biscuits and apples in the bothy and I ate them and slept again. I felt safe for the first time in weeks being inside after sleeping in me van and I was dog tired.

'The kids brought me more snacks and I had a little dog, a Jack Russell, for company. Is he yours?'

'That'll be Arty from Manor Farm. He's always up here.'

'I was feeling more like meself but I didn't know what to do so I decided to hang around and see what'd happen when I was discovered.'

'What did you expect to happen?' asked Izzie.

'I thought you'd either call the police or something would be sorted out.'

'What kind of something?' Kitty wanted to know.

'Maybe you'd hire me as a handyman. It looks as there are several jobs that needed doing.'

Before Kitty could answer Beth's car turned into the yard. Midge and Harry rushed towards the house waving brightly patterned pictures depicting tigers, snakes and blobby people and burst into the kitchen before Beth could halt their charge.

'Joe!' shrieked Midge. 'You've found Mummy!'

'Yes,' agreed Kitty giving her son a hug. 'But you should have told me that he was in the bothy.'

'Joe likes the bothy. He said it is "right cosy" and was "content" to be there.'

'I'd better be going,' said Joe tidying his cups and plate. 'Thank you very much for the breakfast but I'll be off now.'

'Where to?' asked Izzie.

'Dunno,' he laughed. 'I don't expect me Dad's auntie is still around.'

'What was her name?' asked Beth. 'Mark's family have lived here for years so he might have known her.'

'Wagstaff! That's right Minnie Wagstaff,' replied Joe. 'Dad told me how he'd loved the place when he was a little 'un and helped his uncle with the sheep on the Hatherstone Hills. That's what came into me mind when I was out of it. I just wanted to get there.'

'I don't know of any Wagstaffs in the village but I'll ask Mark if you like.'

Kitty had been thinking while she prepared some lunch for Midge and Harry. 'You could stay on if you like as there are jobs that need doing but I'd like to make a couple of calls first.'

Izzie and Beth exchanged glances.

'There'd be talk,' Izzie told her. 'There'd be village gossip if Joe stays in the house.'

'I'd stay in the bothy.'

Kitty was sure Joe was blushing.

'I'll explain it all to Mrs Finchcock and if she approves then the rest of the village will as well,' she told Izzie and Beth.

'I'll talk to Mrs Selby. She doesn't always see eye-to-eye with Mrs Finchcock but she'll be able to stop any tittle-tattle,' Beth decided. 'I'll also ask Mark if there's any labouring going. Have you done any farm work?'

'Not really but I'll have a go at anything.'

'Joe, do you want to contact your daughter?' Izzie asked. 'She must be worried about you.'

Joe's voice dropped to nearly a whisper. 'I'm not sure where she is as she didn't get in touch before Christmas... it was that and the flooding that decided me to leave. The last address and number I had was on my mobile and that was nicked along with my van.'

The only sound in the farm kitchen was the sound of Midge and Harry crunching up apples.

To break the tension Kitty asked Joe if he'd like a shower and shave; an offer that he quickly and gratefully accepted.

'He seems genuine enough.' Kitty told Rollo. 'But could you do a couple of checks for me?' He says he came from Applethwaite in Cumbria where he had his own woodworking business.'

At the other end of the phone Rollo put down the pastrami and pickle sandwich he was having as part of his lunch and began to search the web. 'Did you say Appleby?'

'No, Applethwaite. Appleby is where that Horse Fair is held'

'Ah, here we are. There's a Jacob Saxon & Son listed as bespoke furniture makers in Applethwaite ... and ... an obituary for a Jacob and Mary Saxon.'

'When was that?'

'Four years ago. Look Kitty, are you sure about this? He could have just looked up the names and memorised dates and places.'

'Yes, I am sure.' Kitty paused, 'thanks Rollo, you've reassured me that his story is true. He feels genuine.'

'Well, even so make sure the doors are locked at night and to be on the safe side keep an eye on Sasha and Midge. I'll come up on Friday but promise me you'll ring your dad and let him know what's happening.'

'I'll ring him right away and Rollo, thanks.'

As Kitty rang off Rollo stared out of his office at the Thames as it flowed onwards towards Lambeth Bridge before punching in another number. There were further, more intensive checks he could make on Joseph Saxon.

Chapter 14

Daisies

The lazy May afternoon was full of birdsong and the gentle buzzing of bees in Stoney Lea's lilacs. Ivy and Buddy, gliding like miniature panthers stalked butterflies through the peonies and forget-me-not scattering seeds and petals as they went.

Sasha and Alice, sitting cross-legged on the lawn, were making daisy chains. From inside the walled garden a cock crowed.

'It's so funny we've got Henny and Penny, Molly and Polly, Mucky and Yucky but …'

'Mucky and Yucky?'

'Midge chose Clucky and Lucky but me an' Joe call them Mucky and Yucky. But Yucky has stopped laying and has started cock-a-doodle-do-ing instead.'

'That's because you haven't got a cockerel,' Alice, the farmer's daughter, informed her. 'But you won't get any chicks.'

'But we get eggs and chicks come from eggs.'

'But they have to be special eggs for chicks.

'How do you get them?' Sasha concentrated as she split a particularly tough stalk with her thumbnail. 'Is it is a mummy and daddy thing?'

Alice spread out her daisy chain on her lap as she thought about this, 'Yes, I think so.'

'So we need to get a proper cock-a-doodle-do if we want chicks?'

'Yes or you could buy some,' she paused to obtain maximum effect, 'My Mummy is going to have a baby. It's growing in her tummy.'

'Not in an egg?'

This remark caused giggles before they renewed focusing on the daisies.

'You are so lucky 'cos your lawn grows the best daisies ever. My Daddy hates them and mows them up all the time.'

'Mr Finchcock will be here tomorrow and then they'll all be gone,' Sasha split a daisy stalk with her thumbnail.

'Why does Mr Finchcock still come as Joe has started doing your gardening? Is he making sure Joe is doing it properly?'

'Maybe but they are always talking and drinking tea and eating Mummy's biscuits in the bothy even when she invites them into the house.'

'I heard Mrs Selby say that Joe "knows what side his bread is buttered on" and that "he's got his feet well and truly under the table".'

'But you only put butter on one side of the bread and when Joe eats with us he has his feet under the table like everyone else.'

'Mummy let Harry eat his tea under the table once but he got jam all over the floor and he hasn't been allowed to do it again.'

The two girls giggled as they draped strands of daisies around each other's necks.

'Xav says Joe sometimes has breakfast at the Goat Shed.'

'Why?'

'Dunno. Maybe he likes goat's milk.'

'It is yummy in a crummy-bummy sort of way.'

This caused another set of giggles as they murmured 'crummy-bummy' over and over again until it became a kind of mantra to their daisy chain production.

This suddenly ceased as they heard a clip-clop in the yard.

'There's a pony in the yard?'

'Has your Mum bought you a pony?'

'No,' gasped Sasha, 'but it might be a birthday present.'

'When's your birthday?'

'April.'

'So it would be a late present.'

'Yes … but I haven't asked or even hinted that I want one.'

Daisies cast aside they ran towards the gate in time to see a donkey trotting through the open kitchen door.

'There's a donkey in the kitchen. It is just like the one in *Shrek*,' squealed Sasha not knowing whether to be thrilled or frightened.

Alice ran to close the yard gate, as she knew if a loose animal dashed out into the lane it could be injured or cause an accident before picking up Sasha's discarded skipping rope to use as a halter.

Inside the kitchen the donkey was investigating the fruit bowl crunching up the apples but ignoring the oranges and bananas. It turned its head as Sasha and Alice crept in from the yard.

'Good donkey, nice donkey,' whispered Alice using the tone of voice she'd heard her father use to soothe frightened animals. She clicked her tongue to get its attention but the donkey, ignoring her, started to eat a pear. 'Go and find Joe,' she ordered Sasha. 'And your mum.'

Sasha tiptoed out and raced into the kitchen garden where Joe and her mother were busy among the young tomato plants in one of the greenhouses.

'Mum! Joe! Come quickly. There's a donkey in the kitchen!'

'Don't be ridiculous Sasha. There's no donkeys round here.'

'But Mum there is and it's …'

But at that moment there was a loud "hee-haw!" which sent Joe and Kitty running towards the house.

Sasha was delighted how quickly the donkey seemed to accept them. By the time Joe and her mother arrived Alice had put the skipping rope around its neck and was feeding it some of Kitty's freshly baked shortbread.

'It likes your biscuits Kitty. There weren't any apples or pears left and I thought it was still hungry.'

'That's fine Alice but let's get it out of the kitchen?' Kitty scrutinised her spotless kitchen floor which was, thankfully still unsullied by donkey debris.

Joe took hold of the skipping rope and making reassuring noises gently persuaded the donkey to turn away from the biscuits and go back into the yard. He led it to the outside tap where there was a bucket of water. The donkey drank and drank.

'Shortbread always make me thirsty,' whispered Sasha to Alice. 'They are so dry and crumbly.'

'Where can it have come from?' asked Kitty. 'I don't know of anyone with donkeys around here. Do you know of anyone Alice?'

'Everyone has horses or ponies,' sighed Alice who longed for a pony of her own.

'Can we keep it Mummy?

'I don't think so Sasha as someone must be missing it.'

'Kitty, go and ring the vet as he'll be able to check on the ownership as I reckon it'll be microchipped. Alice, run home and ask your Mum or Dad for some food for it as I think this donkey is really hungry and will need more than biscuits and apples.'

Alice ran down the lane towards Manor Farm and Kitty rang the vet while the donkey nuzzled Joe's hand as if in approval.

'Oh Joe! It likes us. I do hope it can stay,' sighed Sasha pulling a burr off its matted grey coat.

'The vet is on his way,' Kitty stroked the donkey's flank. 'He was just the other side of the village at Prunehill Farm. Look! Here's Mark.'

68

Alice jumped out of her father's mud-splattered Land Rover to open the yard gate. Not only had she returned with her father but with her mother, brother, Midge and Xavier.

As the donkey started to eat the calf nuts Beth had poured into a bowl, Mark took off Sasha's skipping rope and slipped a halter round the donkey's head and tethered it to one of the rings fixed in the wall. 'Well, this is a turn up. You say Max is on his way?'

'Yes, he was only at Prunehill,' said Kitty. 'I hope he'll be able to help us find out where it came from.'

Mark laughed, 'Kitty, it is not an it but a she and I reckon she's in foal.'

'Like Mummy!' shrieked Alice.

'Yes but no,' Beth told her excited daughter. 'I'm not going to have a baby donkey.'

'Midge, come and stroke the donkey,' Kitty urged. 'She'll be fine as long as you're gentle.'

'It's not fair,' grumbled Midge. 'All the exciting things happen when I'm not here and why can't it be a boy donkey?'

'Because it isn't,' Alice told him. 'And if it was it wouldn't be having a foal.'

'Why not?'

But before either his mother or Alice could proffer an explanation, the vet and his even muddier Land Rover turned into the yard.

The donkey was chipped but calls to the owner proved negative as he'd moved on and at the forwarding address he was now unknown.

'There was a Donkey Derby in Oakamoor on Saturday,' said Beth. 'Maybe they've mislaid a donkey.'

'I don't think so,' said the vet as he examined the donkey. 'She's too far gone to have been ridden although it is difficult to work out exactly when the foal is due without a scan as a donkey's gestation can be anything from ten and a half to fourteen months.'

'Nine months was long enough for me,' laughed Kitty.

'And for me!' Beth patted her rounding belly.

'I think she's been on the loose for a while as she's in quite a poor condition. Look at her hooves and her coat. It also looks as if she's had an injury at some time and hasn't had the proper treatment.' Max patted her bulging flank and looked thoughtful. 'I'll go and get my trailer and take her back to the surgery and give her a thorough check. But …' he paused, 'if there's nothing seriously wrong I can't keep her more than overnight. Mark, could you house her?'

'We've got room here haven't we Mummy now Grandpa Ted has taken all his car stuff out of the stables?' Sasha pulled at her mother's arm. 'She can go in there and we'll look after her. Won't we Midge?'

'I'll keep an eye on her as well,' promised Mark. 'Joe, have you had any equine experience?'

'No, apart from a donkey ride on Blackpool beach when I was a lad,' Joe patted the donkey. 'But with Mark's guidance we'll manage.'

'She needs good quality food and plenty of water and some gentle exercise. But I wouldn't leave her untethered or she might take off again.'

While the vet had been examining the donkey, Beth had been busy online. 'Max, there's a donkey sanctuary near Buxton. Could she have come from there?'

'Maybe. Will you give them a ring? Now I'll go and get the trailer.'

'Don't bother, I'll get mine' said Mark. 'It's closer' and he went back to his Land Rover.

'What are you going to call her?' Joe asked Sasha. 'You can't keep on calling her donkey.'

'Daisy!' Xavier pointed to the daisy chains around Sasha and Alice's necks. 'Call her Daisy!'

The donkey brayed as if in approval of her new name.

Chapter 15

A Man in a Car

To Midge the hot, late June afternoon seemed endless. There was no one to play with as his mother was tying up tomatoes in one of the greenhouses and Joe was building new cupboards in his mother's bedroom. Sasha and Xavier wouldn't be home from school until gone three and Harry had gone with his mummy to get some new shoes. Midge kicked at a stone with his old, scuffed ones.

He'd taken a couple of custard creams from the biscuit tin for Daisy knowing Mummy would be cross as the vet had told them that sweet treats weren't good for donkeys although no one had informed Daisy that this was the case.

For once the donkey wasn't interested in the proffered confectionary but continued to walk round and round her stable treading down the straw under her dainty hooves.

There was a great change in her appearance from in the bedraggled, unwanted animal that had trotted into Stoney Lea's kitchen in late May. Her grey coat now shone from Sasha and Alice's daily grooming which emphasised the dark brown cross along her back and withers. Her hooves were now in perfect order after Phil, the farrier's careful attention. Midge stared at her bulging flanks; Sasha had said she'd seen the foal kicking inside Daisy's tummy and Midge longed to see it for himself.

Nobody had come to claim Daisy although a photo of her being fed carrots by Sasha, Midge and Xav had been in the local newspapers. Two donkey sanctuaries had offered to give her a home but it had been decided that she would stay at Stoney Lea with Mark and the vet keeping an eye on her until she'd had her foal or until her real owner turned up.

Usually Daisy would be under the huge oak tree in Stoney Lea's paddock where Mark kept some of his calves while Mabel, a large black and white cow attempted to teach them 'manners'. Daisy was safe there as the paddock was enclosed by dry stonewalls and had a stout five-barred gate. Another important point was that there was no ragwort in the field. Alice had told them that ragwort was poisonous. Deadly, and Daisy must not eat it.

Ragwort. Midge mulled the word over in his mind as he sat on the top step of the old mounting block nibbling the rejected custard creams. He wasn't sure what it looked like but he knew he'd keep Daisy safe and make sure she avoided it if he could.

He was still lost in a vision of himself protecting the donkey from rampant poisonous plants when a big, black car drove down the lane towards Manor Farm.

This was interesting as it was usually only Mark's Land Rover and Beth's little red car or the milk tanker or tractors with their loads of silage or muck that used the lane and once a day the post van bumped along it. Midge climbed on to the yard gate to get a better look, as it was, after all a very big and very shiny car.

He was still hanging on to the gate when the car came back and stopped outside Stoney Lea's gate. The dark glass of one of the rear windows whirred as it was lowered and a man spoke to him.

'*Kisfiú* ... little boy what is your name?'

Midge knew he shouldn't talk to strangers but he was on his side of the closed gate and so he felt safe. For some reason he gave his real name, 'Oliver.'

'Well, Oliver, do you live here?' the man smiled with a flash of gold teeth.

'Yes.' Midge now wished he were safe inside the house or in the greenhouse with his Mummy.

'Do you have any other little boys to play with?'

'Yes.'

'And who are they?'

'I play with Harry.'

Midge didn't like the way the man was smiling at him and felt really frightened when another man got out of the car and opened the rear door. As the man got out of the car and, leaning on a stick, began to walk towards him. Midge felt terrified.

'And where is 'Arry?'

'His Mummy has taken him to buy new shoes.'

'Ah *jó* ... good,' the man smiled again. 'And this 'Arry, this *kisfiú* - he lives 'ere?'

'No,' whispered Midge.

The man began to approach the gate and the other man stepped forward as if to open it. 'Now, *kisfiú*,' said the man, 'tell me where this 'Arry lives.'

Midge, now thoroughly frightened, jumped down off the gate and began to run towards the house yelling the first thing that came into his head, 'Ragwort! Daisy is eating ragwort!'

And, on cue, as if she'd sensed something was wrong, Daisy began to bray.

'Midge? What's up?' Joe ran out of the house still holding a large screwdriver. 'And who the hell are you?'

Kitty came running into the yard from the garden and Midge flew into her arms, 'Mummy! That man wants Harry!'

'Please, excuse me. I am looking for my *unokája* ... my grandson. I was told he *domicisiles* ... live*s* here ... there was a photograph...'

Joe gave Kitty a meaningful look, 'your grandson? What's his name?'

The man shrugged. 'His name could be anything but his mother is *Izabella Blakeney*. You know her?'

Joe replied before either Midge or Kitty could speak. 'There's no one around here with that name and we know everyone as we've lived here for years, eh love?' And he put an arm around Kitty and squeezed her shoulder.

Kitty nodded while Midge just stared at the car relieved that someone else was dealing with this very scary man.

'*Szar*! You are sure? What about this 'Arry?' he nodded towards Midge. 'Your *kisfiú* mentioned him?'

There was a sudden cheerful toot of a horn from Beth's bright red car and she and Harry waved as they drove down the lane towards Manor Farm

'There goes Harry,' said Joe. 'He is as blond as my little lad,' and Joe ruffled Midge's fair hair. 'I expect any grandson of yours would have dark hair. Right? And now please leave as we have work to do.'

Taking a business card out of his wallet the man proffered it. 'If you see *Izabella Blakeney* please give her this.'

Joe made a negative gesture towards the card. 'Sorry, but we can't give it to someone we've never heard of?'

'You are sure you don't know the ... *kurva*?'

'I don't know what you have just said but I don't like your tone of voice so get off our land and if you come back we will call the police.'

The man returned to his car and the driver. As they drove away the white card fluttered out of the car window.

'Stay here nice and calm,' said Joe as they watched the car drive towards the village. When it had gone round Cowpat Corner he turned to Kitty.

73

'Kitty, go and ring Izzie and warn her. Are you on the school run? Just keep Xav out of sight. I'm going to ring Max as I think Daisy is trying to tell us that she's going to drop her foal this afternoon.'

Chapter 16

Izzie's Story

Secure in the stable Daisy's foal suckled contentedly. Max had left with his veterinary equipment and a sense of achievement. Donkey births could be far more difficult than that of the average pony but luckily there hadn't been any of the complications he'd dreaded.

Much to Midge's delight the foal was a jack, which meant that it was a boy. He'd been confused over Joe's suggestion that they called him Kong. This still puzzled him even after his mother explained that it went well with Donkey.

As twilight approached the excitement of the afternoon seemed a long way away. With the children safe upstairs - although Kitty doubted it any of the three would be asleep she carried drinks into the garden where Izzie and Joe were already talking.

'I am so sorry about this afternoon; it must've been a horrible experience for Midge,' said Izzie taking one of the tall glasses.

'I think Kong's arrival has wiped that out,' said Kitty sipping her Pimms. She'd retrieved the card dropped from the car window but the name meant nothing to her. 'The man said he was looking for his grandson.'

'He was looking for Xav,' Joe said reaching out for Izzie's hand. 'He must've been told about the photo of the kids with Daisy and come on the off chance.'

'But we insisted that only the children's first names were in the paper ...'

'I know but Xavier isn't a common name and their ages were there. Maybe he was seeing if there was a connection or someone had informed him that there was a dark haired boy without a father living in Eden Bridge.' Izzie took a long drink and smiled at Kitty. 'I need to give you a proper explanation before I go into school and talk to Mrs Drummond and Xav's teacher.'

Joe put down his glass of ginger beer and squeezed Izzie's hand, 'Go on love; get it off y'chest.'

Izzie began her story. 'I was Isabel Blakeney for twenty-eight years after which I changed my name to Buchann which was my great aunt's name.'

'The artist?' said Kitty, thinking of the wonderful painting of the Hatherstone Hills hanging in Izzie's cottage.

'Yes. After Oxford I was fast tracked into the Civil Service where I was allocated various roles within the Foreign Office ending up eight years ago in Madrid.' She sipped her drink and grinned. 'I had a whale of a time. The work wasn't arduous and there were parties and fun people and ...'

'Dancing on tables?' said Kitty remembering when Izzie had slipped up over her name the previous year.

'Yes ... at times. But then I met Maceo. He was in Spain for the summer; visiting his father who was a big wig attached to the Hungarian Embassy.' Izzie became suddenly serious. 'He was younger than me and still at university but so sweet and funny. Everyone thought I was having a fling – a bit of summer fun but there was more to it than that.

'In September Maceo had to go back to Budapest to finish his degree and I discovered I was pregnant.

'I must admit I was dithering about going through with it when this furious Hungarian turned up at my apartment demanding that I had an abortion and if one word of how I had ruined his only son's life ever got out he would have me *"megsemmisült"*.'

'He'd what?' asked Kitty although she guessed from Izzie's tone that it wasn't something very pleasant.

'Annihilated,' replied Joe. 'Izzie has told me that Tivadar Czinege was and still is a nasty piece of work with dealings and influence in all the wrong places.'

'Right,' agreed Izzie. 'In some quarters the diplomatic service is a useful front for all sorts of shady goings on. Anyway, his threats made me determined to keep the baby although I never told Maceo about my decision.

'I came home where my fanatical kirk-fixated father threw me out and my wonderful aunt in south London gave me and, seven months, later Xav a home.

'We stayed in Putney after she died as she'd left her house and her whole estate to me. When Xav was nearly three we started to get a lot of inexplicable cold callers while our neighbours were left undisturbed. The police weren't interested but I knew something wasn't right and after a woman declaring she was Xav's aunt tried to collect him from nursery I decided it was time to move on and ... if possible disappear.'

'So you came to the Goat Shed?'

'Not straight away. I arranged for an agent to sell the house and put everything in store and we went on our travels; first to Shropshire, then Scotland where my father and his new wife were still not interested in Xav, our situation or me. We stayed with uni friends first in Clitheroe and later in Chester and finally ended up here where we hoped to stay.'

'Why is this man now looking for you?'

'He's looking for Xav not me. For some reason he wants Xav and he is not getting him.'

'But why now?' Kitty was puzzled.

'I don't know. Maybe something has happened to Maceo.'

'I'll ring Rollo! He'll know what to do as he too has ... connections,' and Kitty ran into the house.

Joe gave Izzie a comforting hug. 'Izzie, go and check on the kids and I'll look in on Daisy and Kong and then we'll see what Rollo has to say,' and he kissed the top of her head.

Izzie smiled at him and kissed him back; feeling safe and secure in this new, protective and unlooked for love.

Chapter 17

Kong in the Paddock

When the Finchcock's car turned into Stoney Lea's yard it looked as if a party was going on.

'I hope you don't mind us all turning up uninvited,' said Mrs Finchcock addressing Kitty. 'I was telling Richard and my son, Alex how this was going to be Kong's big day and we just decided to drop everything and come along. I hope it's all right?'

'Of course,' said Kitty, 'the more the merrier but the vet has told us to leave the merriment until after the Big Event.'

'Naturally.' Mrs Finchcock looked round at the assembled group. 'Kitty, I don't think you've met my youngest son. Alex, let me introduce you to Kitty Munroe. Kitty, Alex lives in London and has come home for the weekend.'

Kitty smiled and shook hands with the newcomer. Alex Finchcock was tall with rather angular good looks and a mop of tousled tawny brown hair. Kitty thought he was most likely in his mid-thirties and resembled his parents in that he had his mother's expression of determination and hazel eyes like his father's, which contained the same look of good humour.

Max, the vet came out of Daisy's stable. 'I think we're ready so everyone, quiet please. Mark, if you'll open the yard gate we'll make a start.'

There wasn't the slightest need for Kitty, Beth or Izzie to remind their children to be quiet as Max had carefully explained what might happen if there was sudden noise. So, as quiet as the proverbial church mice, they all watched as the vet led Daisy out of her stable and into the yard. After what seemed a long, tense moment, Kong's long grey nose poked out of the stable doorway.

The three-day-old foal, still unsteady on his spindly legs, looked in wonder as his horizons widened until his mother whickered to him and he began to trot after her. Max led Daisy out of the yard and down the lane to the paddock. Mark had fortuitously moved Mabel and her charge of unruly calves into another field. The spectators to this momentous excursion followed the vet, donkey and foal at a respectful distance.

Once the gate to the paddock was safely shut Max untied the leading rein and stepped back.

To Daisy, who, on Max's recommendation, had been confined to her stable since Kong's arrival, the paddock looked peaceful and inviting. She stared for a moment at the new shelter Joe had built during her confinement before kicking up her heels and galloping off. Kong stood bewildered and called to his mother before trying out a few capers for himself.

By the time Daisy's mad careering was over and she recalled her maternal duties everyone was either sitting on the gate or leaning over the wall watching Kong trying out the freedom and space of his new home.

Kitty's parents took it upon themselves to take the Finchcocks aside and explain that Kitty didn't want any photos on social media or sent to the papers. There'd been enough publicity about Daisy when she'd arrived at Stoney Lea and as her original owner still hadn't materialised Kitty now wanted things, donkey-wise, to have a low profile. Mrs Finchcock, for all her faults, was a very astute lady, and readily agreed.

It had been fortuitous, that when the man in the shiny black car stopped in the village to question a local resident about the whereabouts of *Izabella Blakeney,* it had been her husband that had been waylaid.

Richard Finchcock, respectable in his Panama hat and cream linen jacket and off for an afternoon stroll by the river, had taken an instant dislike to the stranger's officious questioning and especially to his shiny chauffeur-driven car, which had ploughed into the verge outside his house gouging deep furrows into the velvet-smooth turf.

Richard sent him on his way after truthfully pronouncing ignorance of anyone with a name even remotely resembling *Blakeney* living in the area never mind in the village.

Leaving all the children, along with Joe, Richard and Alex Finchcock, watching Daisy and Kong enjoying the freedom of the paddock everyone else went back to the house where there was to be a celebration lunch.

'So Izzie, how are things?' asked Rollo as he carved the ham. 'No more unwanted visitors?'

'Nothing so far but it has been only a few days but I can't help feeling uneasy.'

'That's understandable.' Rollo placed a slice of pink, honey-roast ham on to a large willow pattern plate before coming straight to the point. 'Three months ago Maceo Czinege was injured in a car crash in the States.'

'Oh! The poor boy,' gasped Izzie. 'Is he badly hurt?'

'His life-support machine was switched off two weeks ago.'

Tears welled up out of Izzie's eyes as Rollo put his arm around her.

'I don't know if we would've made it,' she said rubbing her tears away on the lacy hem of her flowing skirt. 'We were never given the chance but ... he was so young and beautiful.'

'Maceo wasn't married and it appears that ...'

'Xav must be the only grandchild and his heir.' Izzie suddenly sat down as the realisation struck her of how this could change their lives. 'Rollo, how can I protect my son? My family has rejected us but my dad is just a self-righteous bigot compared to Maceo's father. I can't and won't let my son be ... influenced or corrupted by Tivador Czinege and his ... detestable way of life. What should I do?'

Rollo thought for a moment. 'As I said I've made some enquiries.' Rollo paused as he wondered how to phrase the next bit of information. 'Let's just say that in some very influential and international quarters people are aware of Tivador Czinege's activities. He's back in Hungary at the moment and I've asked to be informed if and when he comes back to the UK.' Rollo tossed a few scraps of ham to the cats that were weaving round his ankles in great expectation.

'Should we move?'

'I've asked about that and the recommended advice is to stay put but to be on the alert. Let me know immediately and I mean immediately if anything extraordinary happens or there are unexpected changes. Do you know of any Hungarians locally?'

'No ... although Chris and Melissa's au pair might be.'

'Has she been here at Stoney Lea recently?'

'I don't think so. Kitty doesn't see much of any of the Munroes.'

'I'll look into it anyway.' Rollo paused as he thought about the situation until Ivy clawed at his legs eager from more scraps. 'Now, if there's an unusual amount of lost tourists and especially travellers or itinerate workers around let me know straightway.'

He cut some ham into tiny bits for the impatient cats, 'Do you know if Mark uses casual labour?'

'I don't think so.'

Rollo cut another slice of ham before pointing the carving knife at Izzie's flowing pink and cornflower blue patterned, lace edged skirt. 'You could try dressing yourself and Xav a little more conservatively and changing your names; I've heard that "Saxon" might be a possibility.'

Izzie blushed as she kissed his cheek. 'Rollo, you are a good man; not only a true friend to Kitty but now to Xav and me.' Pinching a piece of ham off the serving plate and flicking the fringe of her silvery scarf in Rollo's direction she went to discuss the situation with Joe.

'I used to come up here to play tennis with Mark and the Redman boys' Alex and Kitty were sitting on the lawn, surrounded by plates smeared with the remains of summer pudding and strawberries and ice cream, and watching Sasha and Alice playing with the cats. The rest of the party were either playing a rowdy game of rounders or sitting and enjoying the sunshine in the walled garden. Betty Oxley and Mrs Finchcock were chatting away as if they were old friends as they vied to share their knowledge and opinions on a variety of topics ranging from the proper care of delphiniums to the necessity of using soda water to lift stains.

'It took a while for us to be accepted when Mum and Dad moved to Eden Bridge as my mother can be a bit … forceful but the Redmans were great,' Alex grinned as he thought about how his mother loved to take charge of things. 'They invited us to everything, asked Mum to help with the church flowers and the fête and Dad to join the cricket club until gradually we were part and parcel of village life.'

'That's exactly what your mother did when we arrived,' laughed Kitty wondering if she dared tell him how she'd initially provided the church flowers. 'But she's been a real friend to me and to my family.' Kitty speculated how much Alex knew and decided that his parents would have informed him about her situation. 'After my husband was killed in … an accident she was absolutely marvellous. My parents took good care of the children but I was in pieces.'

It was just more than a year since Tom had died and, although at times Kitty felt that life was getting back to normal, the hurt and that initial sense of loss would come rushing back quite frequently accompanied with raw and painful anger. A sudden feeling of this lingering grief made Kitty's eyes fill with tears but she pushed it away and ran a finger round the rim of the cut-glass dish that had been filled with strawberries.

'The kids and I were staying with friends when it happened as we were having some major electric work done so Tom stayed here for the workmen.

'One morning when the men arrived he wasn't there. His car was in the yard and the house was unlocked. The radio was on in the workshop and that's where they found him under that bloody car. A mug of tea was still lukewarm on the workbench.' Kitty paused and bit her lips before continuing. 'The

81

police think he was reaching out to answer his phone as it was on the workshop floor and he dislodged the jack and his head was …'

Alex reached out and tried to take hold of her hand. 'Don't go on if it is too raw.'

'Raw! It's bloody painful,' Kitty snapped pulling her hand away. 'Oh, I'm sorry but it still hurts. She paused and scrubbed at her eyes and nose with a crumpled napkin before carrying on.

'Tom had bought this wreck of a car, which he and his father were restoring. We'd argued over it as he'd spent all the money we'd earmarked for doing up the house. It ruined all our plans, as we had to stop the renovations except for the absolute basics. He said the car was a rare model and when properly restored would be worth a fortune.'

Kitty shivered despite the bright sunshine. The Jackson-Johnson remained securely locked in the workshop. Joe had said he might know of someone in Cumbria, who might restore it although Kitty knew she'd never recoup the £65,000 Tom had blown on it.

Desperate to change the subject Kitty gestured towards the garden where antique creamy-white roses flowed over the rustic pergola and at the neatly edged lawn and the beds and borders bright with flowers and busy bees. 'Your father comes up every Tuesday and mows the lawn and keeps things in order for us. He was marvellous last year, as the place would've become a wilderness in no time. Joe is now managing the vegetable garden and would do this garden as well but your dad insists that he wants to carry on.'

Alex grinned, as he knew that was typical of his father's innate kindness.

'After the police and forensics decided that it was only the workshop that needed to be isolated, your mother arrived and just took charge of everything, the washing-up, clearing the kitchen and sorting the laundry. Tom had stripped the bed and had loaded the washing machine. The duvet cover, sheets and pillowslips were still in there, creased and damp.' Kitty stopped and watched a pair of peacock butterflies fluttering in the lavender border. 'I don't know why he'd done that as we weren't due back until Friday.'

'Maybe he'd spilt coffee,' Alex suggested.

'Or wine. There were two wine bottles in the recycle bin outside the back door.' Tom had always been very strict about recycling. 'Anyway, your mother was wonderful.'

'She is terrific at getting things done although when we were kids she made me and my brothers really work for our pocket money. We called her "the slave driver".' Alex laughed and Kitty realised that he had real admiration as well as affection for his parents.

'It is beautiful up here,' Alex lay back on the grass. 'London air never feels this fresh and clean.'

'Why live there?'

'Work. I was in the States; in Denver; the "mile high city" until two years ago when my marriage fell apart. After the divorce, which we got in Nevada of all places, I came back to the UK and a friend offered me a job which I took as a stop-gap while I thought about what I wanted to do next.'

'And have you thought?'

'Yes. I want to get a dog again but not while I'm still working in London.'

'We haven't got a dog but sometimes it seems as if we have one,' laughed Kitty. 'Ever since Joe fitted the cat flap Arty, that's Mark and Beth's Jack Russell, is in and out of the house all the time.'

'I know Jack Russell's are small but to get through a cat flap?'

'Arty is somewhat small for the breed but he has an enormous ego. He mastered the cat flap before the cats as they prefer someone to open the door for them – especially Holly.'

'She's called Buddy!' Midge stated crawling out from beneath a cistus scattering pink petals and throwing himself on to his mother's lap.

'But her real name is Holly,' Sasha came over clutching the two squirming cats. 'This one is Ivy and this is …'

'Buddy!' Midge made a grab for the cat-with-two-names but she wriggled out of Sasha's arms and made a dash for the safety of the lavender bushes.

Sasha offered Alex Ivy to hold.

'Hello puss-cat.' He stroked her smooth black fur and tickled her behind her ears and under her chin as she began to purr in feline ecstasy. 'Going by their names I guess they arrived at Christmas time?'

'Yes,' said Kitty, 'and they were a godsend although they caused havoc; not only climbing the Christmas tree but swinging on the fairy lights and sending cards and baubles flying.' She reached over to stroke Ivy. 'But they were a wonderful distraction as it was our first Christmas without Tom.' She gave her children a hug, 'Now, I'm going to put the kettle on and make some tea.'

'Let me help,' offered Alex. 'As I said I'm used to clearing away …'

'And washing up?'

'From a tender age,' Alex grinned as he carried a pile of stacked dishes back into the house.

'On wet afternoons we used to play French cricket in here as there's so much room,' Alex looked round the scullery, 'using a tennis ball of course but Mrs Redman was a very tolerant parent.'

She must've been, thought Kitty as she scraped scraps into the kitchen caddy.

'You haven't changed it.'

'You know the saying "the path to hell is paved with good intentions," Well, that's this scullery.' Kitty rinsed her hands. 'We wanted to keep the farm kitchen as it is and planned to refit this as a utility kitchen for the fridge, cooker and dishwasher and so on. The bathroom was going to become a cloakroom as well as a loo.' Kitty pointed to the other end of the room. 'We'd have made that the laundry area and kept one of the storerooms for boots, wellies and the like. The larder would have stayed the same but the old washhouse would've been turned into Tom' office.' She sighed. 'Everything had to stop as we ran out of cash.' She rinsed the remains of summer pudding off a fruit and cream smeared plate under the tap before putting it in the dishwasher.

'Upstairs it is the same. We couldn't put in the new bathrooms although recently Joe has started building the cupboards in our … in my bedroom but we really need an upstairs bathroom'

'You said that your husband blew the renovation money on a car?'

'Oh yes; it is a rare 1937 Jackson-Johnson which would be worth a fortune if it wasn't a festering pile of scrap mouldering in the workshop.'

'Why don't you get rid of it?'

'I don't know,' Kitty picked up a blue and white striped tea towel and dried a large oval plate before putting it down on the worktop. 'It was the cause of Tom's death. He died, under it, all alone and from a traumatic brain injury.'

She tried to dismiss the image of the last time she'd seen Tom laid out on the slab in the morgue. Rollo had offered to identify him but Kitty had insisted that she should be the one to do it. Tom's father and Rollo had been with her, all three of them needing the support of each other.

The tea towel now resembled a tightly twisted stick of striped Irish linen barley sugar. 'He hit his head underneath that fucking car. When the builders found him he was already dead.

'At first I wanted to smash it into smithereens – eradicate it from the face of the earth because it killed Tom.'

'Please don't go on as I can see it is upsetting you.'

Kitty shook her head. 'I began to think that because the car took away my husband's life and deprived my children of their father it therefore, owed us,' She shook out the crumpled tea towel and gave a wry smile. 'This was brought home to me after Tom's father and brother were inordinately keen to take it off my hands.'

'To sell?'

'Most likely but to their advantage not mine or Sasha and Midge's. So, it is still there locked away in the workshop. I'll ask Joe to show it to you if you like.'

'Thanks but at the moment I'd rather we went upstairs.'

Kitty was taken back. Surely Alex wasn't propositioning her? He'd seemed so nice and friendly.

'Don't get me wrong.'

Was Alex blushing?

'I'm an architect and perhaps between us Joe and I could sort out your problems. Have you still got your original plans?'

Kitty, somewhat relieved, nodded.

'I'd have to consult with your architect but I'm sure we can retrieve something. Do you still use the kitchen staircase?'

Kitty's head was reeling. She'd spoken quite freely about Tom, his horrendous death and that bloody car to a stranger. There was still pain but it had been quite cathartic to talk about it; quite different from the counselling sessions she'd had with the family liaison officer in the summer months following Tom's death.

In that room, decorated to produce a feeling of calm, peace and trust where she'd sworn and sobbed before being advised to "put on a brave face for the sake of the children" before leaving the counselling suite exhausted with sorrow and emotion to "face the world".

The weight of having to carry the grief of her children, Tom's parents and his brother had all but crushed her. Strength had come through her parents and from friends, old and new. Rollo had been a tower of strength while at the same time having to cope with his own grief. Kitty knew she would have really gone under without them.

'Kitty?' called George. 'Your Mum and I are going with Joe and the kids to say goodnight to Daisy and Kong and then we must be going home.'

Izzie was humming tango's most recognisable song, *La Cumparsita* as she entered the scullery and executing what Kitty recognised as a rather slick *promenade, ronde, slip* and *swivel.*

Dancing was also a great therapy, Kitty thought as, closing the fridge door with a flourish; she joined in with the now well-practiced tango routine.

'Kit?' asked Izzie as she accepted a glass of white wine. 'What exactly is it that Rollo does?'

'I don't really know,' admitted Kitty. 'I asked Tom once but he said, "If he told me he'd …"'

'Have to kill you!' Izzie finished off the hackneyed phrase.

'Yes but Tom said he'd mean it.'

'Rollo – a secret agent working for MI6 – keeping our nation safe?' Izzie stopped dancing and looked at Kitty. 'He really loved Tom you know.'

'I know; he always has.'

Izzie hugged Kitty. 'And now he loves you and the children with the same loyalty and devotion as he loved Tom. But I'll tell you something; we should be thankful that he knows a lot of important and very influential people.'

'I know, dear Rollo.' Kitty sniffed and wiped her eyes. 'I seem to be in a yo-yo of emotions today.' She picked up her glass of wine and took a sip. 'Izzie, Alex has offered to talk to our old architect and is coming back next weekend to see about finishing the bathrooms and the scullery.'

'That'll be marvellous! You really need an upstairs loo.'

'He's already spoken to Joe and he thinks they can work together and he'll be able to call in favours from local plumbers and plasterers.'

'Great, good news all round.' Izzie completed a graceful *el giro* turn towards the wine bottle.

Kitty watched and twiddled with the stem of her glass. Izzie was far better at tango that either herself or Beth. Maybe it was all those years working abroad. She took a deep breath. 'He's asked me out.'

'What?' Izzie's dance steps faltered. 'Where? When?'

'To the Chatsworth Balloon Festival. I told him that I wasn't ready to go out with anyone … and, anyway, I was already going to it with you and Joe and the children.'

'Would you have gone if we weren't all going together?'

'Yes … maybe … I don't know. It is too soon if you know what I mean'

Before Izzie could express her opinion Sasha rushed into the scullery, 'Mummy! Grandma and Grandpa want to say goodbye!'

'We'll finish this conversation later,' Izzie informed Kitty as they went back into the kitchen.

Chapter 18

Work in Progress

'Six eggs today!' Kitty was jubilant. 'All because Yucky has started laying again and crowing less.'

Izzie scattered a scoop of corn and threw down a couple of heads of lettuce in the hen run before bolting the door and following Kitty into the vegetable garden.

The wooden bench, placed by the high wall looked inviting. Izzie and Kitty, accepting the invitation, sat and admired the labour of others.

'Everywhere you look there is an absolute abundance,' Kitty stretched out her arms to soak up the sun.

All around the vegetable garden were the fruits of Joe's, Mr Finchcock's and, to some extent, her own labours. The strawberries and gooseberries were just about finished but the raspberries were at their peak; safe from thieving birds in their sturdy fruit cage. Netted red, white and blackcurrants were ready for picking. The espalier fruit trees along the garden walls were filled with: plums, greengages, apples, pears and quince.

The rows of runner beans were brilliant with scarlet flowers while on beds of straw courgettes were perceptibly swelling day-by-day. The other beds were just as full with: carrots, cauliflowers, potatoes, sweet corn, artichokes and spinach.

'You should get some bees,' observed Izzie.

'Mr Finchcock has mentioned it and has suggested letting a local beekeeper put some hives in the garden but there's Midge ... '

Izzie nodded; Midge was still a busy, inquisitive child. 'School for him when the September term starts.'

'I know,' Kitty smiled and waved her hands towards the garden. 'Tell you what Izzie, I think I'll need another freezer to hold all this bounty.'

'Won't that spoil Alex's grand plan? You wouldn't want it to look out of place among the solid alder Shaker-styled units which will soon be installed in your revamped scullery.'

'Izzie!' Kitty laughed picking up inquisitive Ivy who was investigating the egg basket. 'You know the freezer will be in the storeroom and not hidden behind by one of Joe's beautiful unit doors.'

Kitty was surprised how swiftly events had moved on since Joe and now Alex had come into their lives.

For a start there was Joe and Izzie.

Kitty wasn't exactly sure when their relationship had become something more than friendship. It was now obvious, that it had developed into a loving, happy relationship. Joe still slept in the bothy for Xav's sake but the little boy seemed happy to share his mother with Joe and was often seen, chatting away as they pottered about in either Stoney Lea's or the Goat Shed's garden.

Then there was Daisy and Kong. Ever since the donkey had arrived both the vet and Phil, the farrier kept on turning up at Stoney Lea initially to check on Daisy or on how Kong was progressing and then lingering to drink tea and chat. On one occasion Max had called in on the pretext of wanting to inspect the hens. Kitty had the feeling that they might, just might be, more interested in her.

Both in turn had hinted that if she were interested in going to the balloon festival they'd be happy to accompany her. As it happened, Alex had joined their party – at Mark and Beth's invitation.

Kitty knew she had to give Alex Finchcock some serious thought. He was now visiting Eden Bridge every weekend although spending more time at Stoney Lea than with his parents.

It was because of Alex that the long postponed renovations were under way. He'd met Rollo in London and over a constructive sake and sushi dinner Kitty's finances and a revised estimate for the renovations had been discussed and a budget agreed on. Alex had also contacted the original architect who was happy for him to take over the project.

Since then things had moved on. Her bedroom had been refitted with cupboards and an old school friend of Alex's had started on the plumbing for the new bathrooms so it was hoped that everything including the scullery, cupboards and storerooms would be finished and in full use by Bonfire Night.

For the children to have an upstairs bathroom and an en suite for guests and for Kitty, to have her own shower and loo, would be absolute bliss

Then there was the Jackson-Johnson. The source of so much resentment, misery and, ultimately, bereavement and the ensuing suffering for Kitty and the children, was scheduled to leave Stoney Lea at the end of the next week.

Once again this was due to Joe.

Izzie had persuaded him to go back to Applethwaite to check on his house and workshop and to settle his debts and generally reassure people that he was alive and well. She and Xav had gone with him and it was while he was

89

showing them the beauty and attractions of Cumbria that he had a brainwave about what to do with the car.

Kitty had taken the children down to Manor Farm the afternoon Joe removed the three padlocks and shot back the bolts to open up the doors.

The workshop had been closed ever since the forensic team had left. Her father and Rollo had done a basic tidying up but there was still a lot of rubbish and debris to be disposed of.

Squatting neglected in the gloom and dust for more than a year hadn't improved the old car's appearance; unless you were a student of arachnology or happy for those generations of mice that had been able to grow up in its environs.

Through all the months that the car had caused friction and discord, Tom and his father had been slowly and surely bringing it back from a rusting wreck of assorted parts vaguely attached to an axle to something that was on the way to resembling an elegant, stylish classic vehicle in spite of the paintwork and the upholstery still being in a terrible state.

There was still a great deal of work to be done. Joe knew his mechanical skills were not up to carrying on Tom's work - nor did Kitty want any further restoration done at Stoney Lea.

Joe cleared up the place as best he could; throwing out dried up tins of grease and piles of oily rags. Several mould ridden unwashed coffee mugs made him retch and Joe tried to convince himself by imagining that maybe they contained the serum for a disease that was currently incurable. He dusted away the cobwebs and brushed up mouse dropping before photographing the car from every possible angle. Making sure he'd shooed out the two overexcited mousers he once more triple-locked the doors.

Joe's next task was to go through the Jackson-Johnson's documents and provenance and do some serious research before contacting Rollo.

The car had cost Tom £65,000 as well as his life. Even in its present state, Joe's research showed; because of the rarity of the year, collectors, it appeared, would be willing to pay anything up to or above a quarter of a million pounds for a 1937 Jackson-Johnson.

Joe had a long conversation with Rollo who suggested giving Kitty options on the car's future but not yet to tell her of the car's prospective value.

Chapter 19

The Jackson-Johnson's Future

At two-fifteen on a hot July Saturday afternoon Ted and Simone Munroe drove into Stoney Lea's yard.

Kitty was surprised as Simone and Ted had been seldom visited Stoney Lea since she and Rollo had stopped Ted and Chris from removing the Jackson-Johnson. Invitations to Sasha and Midge's birthday teas, Easter lunch or even to drop in and meet Daisy and Kong had been refused usually on the flimsiest excuse. Likewise, invitations for Kitty and the children to visit them had not been forthcoming. A courier had delivered presents for the children and Kitty's last birthday had been completely overlooked.

Chris Munroe had brought his sons over to see the donkeys but the visit hadn't been a success. Daisy, recognising in Tristan and Dominic, boys who, given half a chance, would pull her tail and throw stones became very protective of her foal.

To demonstrate her disapproval Daisy had bared her teeth, "hee-hawed" loudly before kicking out her heels and leading Kong off into the furthest corner of the paddock. Not even Sasha shaking a bucket of Daisy's favourite dried sugar beet nuts and Midge offering carrots could persuade her to let Tristan or Dominic anywhere near Kong.

'Maybe Holly and Ivy had warned her to keep Kong away from them,' commented Sasha after her uncle and cousins had left. The cats immediately hid whenever the twins visited, no doubt remembering the painful experiences they'd experienced when they were kittens. This afternoon they'd disappeared into their favourite hidey-hole in the fire space underneath the brick copper in the old washhouse. For their feline comfort Sasha had brushed it out and put in a couple of cushions.

This Saturday Kitty wasn't happy to see her in-laws as a swimming party had been planned and Sasha, Midge, Alice and Harry were raring to go. Beth, now five months pregnant was finding the hot weather tiring and an afternoon with her feet up was literally what the doctor had ordered.

'Sasha! Oliver! Darlings, how you have grown! Come and give Granny a hug.'

Sasha put down her backpack and allowed her grandmother to hug her while Midge, outraged that he'd been called "Oliver" in front of Alice and Harry scowled before accepting his hug and kiss, while still hanging on to his swimming bag.

"Hello Kitty.' Ted Munroe gave her a kiss. 'You're looking well.'

'Hello Ted, Simone ... lovely to see you but I wish you'd rung as I'm taking the children swimming.'

'They won't mind if we just stay for a cup of tea; will you darlings?' Simone gave the four children now all clutching swimming bags a wide smile. 'You run along and play while Mummy makes Granny a nice cup of tea.' The children stood there wondering what was expected of them. 'Run along and play,' ordered Simone making shooing movements, 'Granny and Grandad won't keep Mummy very long.'

As Kitty moved to unlock the kitchen door she noticed Ted Munroe eying up the padlocks on the workshop.

'Sasha, please run and tell everyone that I'm making tea.'

Sasha looked at her mother and then her grandparents and ran off into the garden followed by Midge, Alice and Harry.

'Oh, what sweet cats!' cooed Simone noticing the cats curled up with Arty on the kitchen windowsill. 'But I didn't know you'd got a dog!'

'We haven't.' Kitty put the kettle on to the Aga's hotplate. 'Arty lives at Manor Farm; he pops in now and then through the cat flap to eat the cat's food.'

Arty, chasing rabbits in his sleep, took no noticed of the visitors.

'You're becoming quite the country girl,' laughed Ted sitting at the kitchen table. 'Rural life seems to suit you. Next you'll be finding yourself a nice gentleman farmer.'

'Ted!' Simone snapped, glancing at some of the clutter left on the kitchen table before moving it aside. They were there for a purpose and upsetting Kitty with tactless remarks wasn't going to help. 'No milk for me please Kitty - just lemon.' She nodded in a meaningful way at her husband.

'Sorry,' mumbled Ted. He stirred his tea before clearing his throat. 'Humph, I heard that ... I mean a little bird told me that you're thinking of selling the Jackson-Johnson. Right?'

'Such a wise decision Kitty,' Simone remarked before Kitty could reply. 'We all miss Tom, you know,' she dabbed her eyes with a Swiss lace-edged handkerchief, 'but it is time to move on dear.'

'Kitty love, has anything been decided about the car?'

Kitty looked into the depths of her teacup before speaking. 'You are right; it is time to move on and having that car in the workshop is a constant reminder for the children … and for me. So, yes, it is going.'

Ted lent forward, visibly eager, 'Is it sold?'

'I am going to …'

'Kitty love, please let me have it. I'll give you what Tom paid for it and …

'Then you'll be able to make the house into the dream home you and Tom planned.' Simone gestured towards the scullery door, 'I noticed when you fetched the milk that you still haven't modernised your working kitchen.' Simone couldn't bring herself to say "scullery". 'The only bathroom is still downstairs?'

'At the moment.'

'How awkward for you and for the children to have to traipse up and downstairs all the time. Kitty, take my advice and accept Ted's offer and let him finish the work that Tom started. It would be a grieving father's memorial to his dear son.'

Kitty felt angry tears pricking her eyes. In her mind Sasha and Midge were Tom's real memorial. Midge had Tom's eyes and inquisitive mind while Sasha had his determination and sense of fun. Both children had coped extraordinarily well with losing their father in spite of the lack of attention and support they'd had from their paternal grandparents. Kitty smelled greed seeping out from both Ted and Simone. She had never really liked them the way she had loved Tom.

Before she could answer, the children ran back into the kitchen followed by Joe. Their chatter woke Arty. The fox terrier, annoyed at being disturbed in what he considered to be his second home, began to bark. He wasn't venting his displeasure at Joe or the children, now rifling the biscuit tin, but at Simone and Ted.

'Who are you?' Simone wanted to know.

'Joe Saxon; a friend,' said Kitty ushering Arty and the children back into the yard. 'Joe is staying with us at the moment and helping me with the car's negotiations.'

'Negotiations? Are you qualified? You look more like a gardener than a negotiator!' Simone was not impressed by Joe's appearance as he was wearing a T-shirt, which had seen better days and faded shorts with twine and gardening gloves sticking out of a pocket.

'Aye, I am that as well,' grinned Joe accepting a mug of tea. 'Has Kitty told you about the car?'

'I was just going to.' Kitty was relieved that Joe was there. 'The car is going to the Brooklands Museum in Surrey.

'What?'

'Surrey? Why on earth?'

'When I decided it was time for it to go, Joe began to do some research. He told me about the Brooklands Museum and that made me think. If the 1937 Jackson-Johnson is such a rare car ...'

'It is, it is,' Ted couldn't keep the enthusiasm of a true classic car fanatic out of his voice.

'I decided that it should be available for as many people as possible to see and enjoy.'

'But it is worth a small fortune.' Covetous greed now tinged Ted's voice as well as his genuine love of motorcars.

'I know that, now.'

'What does Roland say about all this? After all he was Tom's executor?'

'Roland thoroughly approves,' said Rollo entering the kitchen along with Mark, Izzie and Xav. 'Hello Simone - Ted. Yes, the mechanics and experts at Brooklands will be completing the Jackson-Johnson's restoration before it takes pride of place in their brand new display room between a 1936 Auburn Eight Supercharged Speedster and a 1938 Packard Twelve convertible sedan.'

The stunned look on Ted's face made Kitty want to laugh out loud.

'The 1930s was a very special decade for the museum's director so they want to celebrate it in style.' The expression on Rollo's face was, as enigmatic as the *Mona Lisa*'s quite unlike that of Ted and the calculating Simone. 'Kitty's Jackson-Johnson will fit in like a dream. Right Kitty?'

Kitty nodded.

'You're not donating it? Tom paid £65,000 for it and Ted ...'

'Kitty has come to an arrangement with the museum that is satisfactory on all accounts,' Rollo continued. 'However, she is well aware that you, Ted, helped Tom to begin the restoration and therefore has decided to make a one-off reparation in acknowledgement of the encouragement and experience you contributed to the initial work.' Rollo gave Ted and especially Simone a sincere smile. 'Kitty wasn't expecting you today but Ted, we need to make an appointment for you and Kitty to sign the paperwork – and for it to be witnessed.'

'Is that really necessary?' Simone was outraged. She had known Rollo since he and Tom were at prep school and now he was treating them as if they were conniving crooks ready to cheat their beloved daughter-in-law and dearest grandchildren out of a fortune.

She glared at Kitty, 'I suppose you'll squander your profit on this place and spoiling our grandchildren. I knew the moment that Tom brought you home that you'd be trouble.'

'Simone, it's time we were going.' Ted, recognised that his wife was gearing herself up for a full-blown row, held out his hand to Kitty and then to Rollo. 'That'll be fine. Fix a date and we'll get it sorted and finished.

'Come on Simone. It is time to go home.'

But before they could leave four soaking wet children and a small dog rushed into the kitchen. Having realising that the chance of a swim that afternoon had disappeared they had switched on the garden hose.

Simone's simmering rage was not improved by being hugged by her whooping, sopping wet granddaughter.

Chapter 20

Melissa in the Scullery

The plumber was belting out his favourite Elvis song, Vegas-style, as he fitted the shower tray in an en suite bathroom. Since he became enlightened at the age of fifteen Danny Morland had modelled himself on The King; completely disregarding the good intentions of his friends who told him that cultivating thick sideburns and continually combing pints of malodourous grease into his hair to make a quiff made him look like a prick.

One of these friends was Alex Finchcock and the reason why Danny was, happily singing away while he worked on Stoney Lea's guest bathroom.

Ever since Tom had bought the Jackson-Johnson work on the new bathrooms and renovating their bedroom had stopped. The new breeze-block walls and doorways were already in place before Tom's catastrophic accident but the newly created spaces remained unfinished.

Tom had been adamant in refusing to increase their mortgage or taking Kitty's parents offer of a loan, as he was completely confident that they would, in time, recoup his investment 'in spades' as he put his faith in the appeal of a beautifully restored Jackson-Johnson to classic car enthusiasts and collectors. But at that moment they were skint.

In the months following Tom's death Kitty's parents had renewed their offer of a loan but she had been too numb with grief to consider having workmen back in the house with their cheery music and demands for endless cups of tea liberally laced with multiple spoonfuls of sugar. Even Rollo, as Tom's executor and fully aware of Kitty's financial position, hadn't pushed her into getting the bathrooms completed.

It was Joe and Alex's arrival that had changed the situation.

Joe, perhaps as reparation for 'squatting' in the bothy, had offered to build and fit the cupboards in Kitty's bedroom. An offer she readily accepted.

Since they'd moved into Stoney Lea her clothes had been squashed into two small chests of drawers or crammed into the huge but rickety wardrobe her father and Tom had dismantled and transferred from the workshop.

Now the room was furnished with pale oak fitted drawers and shelves, mirrors, a dressing table unit and plenty of cupboard space all cleverly utilising the room's sloping eaves.

Kitty appreciated, on a daily basis, the orderliness of her bedroom and the joy of wearing clothes smelling of lavender and sandalwood. The Redmans had stored paint tins and brushes in the old wardrobe. Even after a thorough scrubbing and repainting the smell of paint and turpentine had lingered although, to be fair, there hadn't been a problem with moths.

Now, thanks to the sale of the Jackson-Johnson there was more than enough money to finish the bathrooms and end night time loo trips down the stairs.

While Danny was singing along in the guest en suite Kitty and Midge were visiting the village school in readiness for September when Midge would join the reception class.

While Midge was listening to a story about *Bogamus the Troll* with the rest of his prospective classmates, Mrs Finchcock, in her role as a school governor, invited Kitty and the other mums to join her and Mrs Drummond, the headteacher, for tea and a chat in the school hall.

A bond of friendship had grown between Kitty and Mrs Finchcock; cemented by the everyday kindnesses Kitty received in the months following Tom's death. On one occasion, Mrs Finchcock, in her practical, down to earth manner had informed Kitty that "widows either, survive, thrive or die" and it was up to her to decide which one she'd be. This had initially upset Kitty but it had made her determined to do more than just survive.

In spite of their growing friendship, Kitty still preferred to call her Mrs Finchcock rather than Esther as she had been instructed to do on numerous occasions.

At half-past two Danny went down the kitchen stairs to make another brew. It would be hard to say who was the most surprised, Danny or the slim, dark haired woman on her hands and knees shining a torch underneath one of the oak dressers.

'Who the fucking hell are you?' Danny demanded, eyeing the trim behind encased in tight blue jeans as the intruder struggled to her feet.

'I could ask you the same question.'

'I asked first,' Danny removed his phone from his back pocket. 'A straight answer or I'm ringing the police.'

'There's no need for that; I'm Mrs Munroe's sister-in-law; Melissa Munroe. And you are?'

97

'Danny Morland, I'm the plumber; fitting the new bathrooms.'

'I heard that Kitty had finally got round to finishing the renovations,' Melissa switched on her best smile. 'Danny, would you like some tea?'

Although Danny was in dire need of a brew he needed to know if the woman filling the kettle in the scullery was who she said she was and more importantly how she'd got in.

'Mrs Munroe never said she was expecting visitors.'

'I'm hardly a visitor,' laughed Melissa. 'Kitty knows I drop by now and again. Sugar?'

'Two please.' But Danny, with the strains of *Suspicious Minds* still echoing in his head, wasn't going to be distracted. 'I'd like to know how you got in as I know both the kitchen and the backdoor were locked.'

'I used the spare key.' Melissa indicated a key tied to a piece of red twine threaded through a cotton reel lying on the kitchen table. 'As I said, I'm family so I know where it's kept.'

'And where is that?'

'There's a space behind one of the stones in the wall to the right of the garden gate. But you mustn't tell anyone.' Melissa's smile became even more seductive, 'It's a big secret. Have you tried Kitty's shortbread? They really are delicious.'

Although Danny took one of the proffered biscuits he still wasn't satisfied.

'And what were you looking for?'

'An earring; I thought I might have dropped it the last time I was here.'

'And when might that have been?'

'It was when the baby donkey was born. We came to see darling little Tong - such a cutie. Have you seen him?'

Danny nodded. Midge and Sasha had dragged him over to meet Daisy and Kong within minutes of his arrival at Stoney Lea to talk to Kitty and Alex about the bathrooms. Tong? Something definitely wasn't right.

'Have you found it?'

'Unfortunately no, but I haven't looked in the back kitchen so maybe I dropped it in there when I was helping with the washing-up.'

Danny looked at Melissa's beautiful hands with their glittering rings and perfect scarlet nails. They didn't resemble any hands he'd seen dealing with dishes. 'Kitty will be home soon so you can ask her if she's found it.'

'Kitty? I really can't hang about as I must … pick my boys up from school.'

'She'll be here in a minute but as you're in a hurry.' Danny picked up the key; 'I'll give this back to her.'

Melissa's smile waivered as she grabbed her bag and ran back to her car; scattering gravel and muck as she roared road Cowpat Corner.

Kitty stared at the key. Two-and-a-half years ago she'd threaded that piece of red twine through the cotton reel and securely knotted it before she and Tom had placed it behind the loose stone just as Mrs Redman had recommended. She hadn't seen it since that day. No one else had needed to know about it as Rollo had his own key and after Tom's accident Kitty had given Izzie and her parent's keys.

'Melissa was in the kitchen?'

'Yeah.'

'And the key was here on the table?'

'Yeah. She was looking under the dresser for an earring.'

'An earring?'

'She said she'd lost it when she came to see the baby donkey.'

Kitty sat down and Ivy immediately jumped on to her lap. She was by far the more demonstrative of the two cats. Sasha had a theory that it was because she had just the one name and therefore knew who she was. Kitty thought hard as she stroked her.

It was just Chris and the two boys who'd come to see Kong. Melissa hadn't been to Stoney Lea since just before Joe turned up and that was after Easter – in late April. So the earring thing was a lie - in fact a double lie as she'd referred to him as …?

'Tong. Now that would be a stupid name for a donkey.' Privately Danny thought Kong was a ridiculous name but then he hadn't played many computer games in his youth preferring to go fishing or making model aeroplanes until he'd discovered Elvis. Now, it was as if, for him at least, the man from Memphis had never left the building.

How did Melissa know about the spare key? In fact Kitty had forgotten all about it. Thick aubrietia now grew over that part of the wall.

Pushing Ivy off her knee Kitty went out into the yard. By the gate to the garden some of the trailing blue-flowering plants had been pulled away revealing a cavity large enough to conceal a key and a cotton reel. Kitty picked up the dislodged piece of stone and pushed it back into the hole.

Someone had shown Melissa the key's hiding place and it hadn't been her.

Traces of Melissa's unauthorised visit still lingered in the kitchen even though Kitty had opened the windows and left the door wide open. *Kotys* - the scent she always drenched herself in - was overpowering and far too sweet for Kitty's taste. Tom knew she loved *Clarabelle's* light, floral tones but had bought her a bottle of *Kotys* after one of his business trips. He'd gone to … Zurich and missed the village fête and … Chris and his boys had come round the next day because Melissa was still in … Zurich.

She'd been wondering how Melissa had known about the key when it came to her, like the proverbial lightning flash. Her sister-in-law and her husband had been having an affair.

The shock of the realisation made her legs tremble and she had to sit down on the kitchen Chesterfield. How often had Melissa let herself in while she and the children had been away or out for an afternoon when Tom was working at home? The thought of Melissa unlocking the door to wait for Tom made Kitty's stomach squirm.

The idea of them having sex in their home or even in their bed made her rush, retching, to the scullery sink.

Sipping some water, Kitty began to wonder what Melissa was looking for and why now, so long after Tom's death. Suddenly there were a lot of questions that she wanted answered.

'So, the broomstick babe let herself in with the secret key and Danny Boy discovered her looking for something?' Izzie poured herself another glass of wine. 'God, this is good. I'm not drinking at home to support Joe.' She put down her glass and looked round the kitchen. 'When did you last move the dresser?'

'We haven't. Dad and Tom tried when we first moved in and we were painting the kitchen. Even when it was empty it was too heavy so we painted round it. I expect it hasn't been moved for centuries and the original lime wash will be still on the wall behind it complete with equally ancient graffiti.'

'You've looked underneath it?'

'Nothing there; except a few dead spiders, some ancient fluff, a couple of pens and a few bits of Lego.' Kitty sipped her wine. 'It would help if we had a clue of what's she's looking for.'

'It must have been lost some time ago.'

'While Tom was alive.'

'Had you any idea they were … y'know?'

'No.' Kitty had been thinking about this ever since Danny had told her about the key. 'Immediately after Tom died it was difficult to take everything in but there were some things that puzzled me.'

'Such as?'

Kitty bit her lip before she spoke. 'He'd stripped the bed and the sheets were still damp in the washing machine and I found one of the new cream bath towels hanging behind the bathroom door and ... there were two peach stones under our bed.'

'All signs that he'd been up to no good; anything else?'

'Three buttons on the bedroom floor; one of them was pearl.'

'Ripped off in the throes of passion? Anything else?'

'I can't remember but ... when Tom said he had meetings in London or Seattle or wherever it could've been an excuse to screw Melissa as she used to go abroad to see clients. I bet you the bastards even did it in a hired classic car.' Kitty's anger began to reappear, 'He bought me a bottle of the same bloody perfume she wears and tried to make me use it.'

'*Kotys* - ah, trying to camouflage his guilt! Did you?'

'No but I opened it as Sasha wanted to try it but even at the peak of her pink-princess phase, she said it smelt like, "penguin poo".'

'Very apt, you've got a very perceptive daughter.' Izzie took another sip of wine. 'I think the reason why Melissa is looking for whatever it is now – is because something has changed. Maybe she thinks it'll be discovered and awkward questions asked and answers demanded.' Izzie put down her glass. 'Kitty, what's changed which might have panicked her into breaking in.'

'Recently - there was Joe in the bothy, Daisy's arrival, the man in the car, Kong's party which the Finchcocks gate-crashed.'

'Joe making your bedroom cupboards and he and Alex planning to revamp the scullery and back kitchen and Joe making enquiries about getting rid of the car.'

'That's it – the Jackson-Johnson!'

'Kitty, Melissa was looking in the kitchen not the workshop.'

'No!' Kitty jumped up spilling her wine. 'I've got it! Chris discovered that the Jackson-Johnson was going when he brought his boys to see the donkeys. He told his dad ...'

'And Ted and Simone visited you.'

'The plans for the scullery were among the mess on the kitchen table and Simone asked me if that was what I intended squandering the money from the car on.'

'So, she must've told Melissa ...'

' ... And Melissa knew she had to find whatever it is before it is discovered and her infidelity revealed.'

101

'But how did she know Midge and I would be out?' Kitty wondered. 'If she'd been lurking on the off chance someone would have noticed her flashy car.'

'Got it!' Izzie leapt up and grabbed her phone. 'Look Kitty; the Mischief Maker has been doing some detective work. Look at the school's website - Induction Afternoon for Prospective Reception Year Intake.'

'She knew Midge's age and worked out that we'd be visiting the school.'

'And used the secret key so she could search.' Izzie grabbed Kitty's hands and laughing they danced a sort of tango round the kitchen.

'But we still don't know what it is.' Kitty was breathless.

'Yes, but we know where to look.' Izzie looked at her watch. 'I'd better be getting back to Joe and Xav. See you tomorrow and we'll search until we find it and Kitty …you'd better mop up that spilt wine.'

Chapter 21

Found

Outside, rain lashed against the windows but inside Stoney Lea's kitchen a profound discussion was in progress.

'So,' said Kitty pouring coffee, 'We'll divide the scullery, storerooms, larder, the bit in the middle and the old washhouse between us and look in every cupboard, on every shelf and along every beam until we find whatever it is. Agreed?'

'Agreed, but I wish I knew what we're looking for.' Joe was still unsure why he'd been roped in for this mysterious grown-up treasure hunt.

'So do we, Joe but when we find it we'll recognise it,' laughed Izzie. 'It'll be a bit like playing hunt the thimble.'

'Is it thimble sized or bigger?'

'We don't know but there'll be a prize for whoever finds it,' promised Kitty.

'And if its you - it will definitely be worth winning!' Izzie gave Joe a kiss.

'Right. I'll take the sink area and look around the washing machine and fridge.'

'Not sure if I like the idea of you revealing the state of my cupboards and drawers to one and all,' Kitty laughed. 'I was half tempted to get up early and clean them out before you all came but that would've defeated the purpose.' Kitty tucked her hair behind her ears and tried to appear businesslike.

'Joe, please will you take the bigger storeroom and I'll start on the larder.'

'Good idea as Joe can make sure there'll be room for the second freezer while he's at it.'

'Izzie!'

'What second freezer?'

'Just one of our little …'

'Feeble jokes but I'll sweep up at the back of the fridge for you if you like,' laughed Izzie opening up the cupboard under the sink.

Kitty fetched a stepladder and gazed around the larder. As usual it felt cool as it faced north and the high window let in very little light or heat, even on the hottest day. The shelves were made of huge stone stabs and reached up in graded tiers to the ceiling. During their first year she had industriously filled those shelves with jars of homemade jam, chutney and pickles.

Last year, after Tom's death, she hadn't felt like stirring simmering vats of blackberries or green tomatoes and her eyes were frequently filled with tears without the help of pickling onions or red cabbage. It was the aching, never-ending loneliness. She'd just wanted to be elsewhere; away from the memories and realisation that Tom had gone. Forever.

But, this year it would be different; as she was determined that chutneys and pickles would once again join the jars of strawberry and blackcurrant jam she'd already made.

'Anyone found anything,' called Izzie putting Kitty's pans back into a cupboard.

'No, but there are some old jelly moulds the Redmans left which I'd forgotten all about.'

'Nothing in the storeroom,' Joe emerged putting his measuring tape back in his pocket. "But if you really need a second freezer there be plenty of room with just a little adjustment to the plans.'

'Well, I found these at the back of a cupboard,' Izzie held up a champagne bottle and two glasses.

'My missing champagne flutes! I thought they'd been broken.'

'We could send then for DNA analysis,' Izzie was pleased to have discovered something. 'But I don't think they are what that hussy Melissa was looking for.'

Kitty suddenly felt very upset; the glasses had been a wedding present from Rollo's parents. To cover her discomfort she asked her friends if they'd like more coffee.

'That'll be lovely. I'll check on the kids while you are doing it.' Izzie left the scullery.

'Kitty, Alex said you'd decided what you want to do with the washhouse,' said Joe looking through the door. 'It's a good size.'

'It hasn't been used for years but Holly and Ivy have started hiding in the copper's fire hole.' She looked round at the flaky, whitewashed walls. 'When we moved in we found an old wooden washing dolly and washboard tucked away in that corner.

'Tom intended using it for his office so he could ...' Kitty paused, 'work at home.' The phrase now had a bitter ring to it. 'Alex thinks I should keep it as a kind of office and workroom for household accounts, the computer and printer etcetera.'

'That'll work.' Joe visualised cupboards and a workstation blending in with the units he'd be building in the scullery and storeroom.

'Kitty, Mrs Finchcock and Alex are here,' Izzie called from the kitchen. 'And I've given the kids juice and biccies in front of the telly and Danny yet another cup of tea. OK?'

'Hello Joe, Kitty I hope you don't mind us dropping in,' Mrs Finchcock put down a bunch of pink and white sweet peas. 'Richard picked these for you this morning just before the heavens opened.'

'Ma would like to see your bedroom Kitty,' said Alex, accepted a cup of coffee. 'She wants to convert the attic into a guest suite and because of the slope of the roof ...'

'It'll need properly fitted cupboards.' Mrs Finchcock stirred her coffee. 'And I've heard that Joe has done wonders in your room.'

Kitty was frantically trying to remember if she had made the bed that morning and if yesterday's dirty clothes were safely in the linen basket. 'We're having a bit of a sort out this morning as ... someone has lost something and we're trying to find it.'

'Where are you looking? Maybe we can help,' Mrs Finchcock put down her cup. 'Alex is brilliant at finding things - it's a kind of gift.'

Alex grinned at Kitty as they followed his mother into the scullery.

'Ah! You've found the glasses. I washed them and put them in a cupboard after the ... accident, as I didn't know where they went,' Mrs Finchcock smiled at Kitty, 'and I didn't want to trouble you over a minor matter when you had so much to contend with.

'And at the time I couldn't find where the recycling bin was kept so I put the bottle in with them. Kitty, my dear is anything wrong?'

Kitty shook her head unable to speak, as the reality of Tom's infidelity became a fact.

'There were other bits and pieces as well,' Mrs Finchcock continued. 'Mostly food debris – scraps of smoked salmon, a couple of lobster tails, some oyster shells, salad leaves, strawberry stalks, a couple of peaches - I just threw everything away.'

'Seems as if someone had a great picnic,' Alex laughed until he saw the look of pain that was crossing Kitty's face.

'More like food for illicit lovers feasting on fishy aphrodisiacs.' Izzie glared at Alex as she put an arm around Kitty's shaking shoulders.

'Sorry, I didn't realise.' Having heard of the circumstances of Tom's death from his mother Alex now felt embarrassed over his untimely remark.

'Was there anything else?' Izzie asked.

105

'Um yes,' Mrs Finchcock hesitated. 'There was something which I didn't think entirely appropriate considering the circumstances so after I'd washed it I tucked it away out of sight.'

'Do you remember where?'

'Of course.'

They all trooped after Mrs Finchcock as she led the way into the washhouse.

'It was too big for any of the cupboards so I put it in here' she said lifting the lid off the old copper.

Reaching inside the she lifted out a large circular object wrapped in one of Kitty's blue and white stripy tea towels.

Disturbed from their morning nap Holly and Ivy emerged from the copper's fire hole and, as the lid had been removed, leapt up to investigate the cast iron liner and consequently, got in everyone's way.

'I think we'd better have a look at this in the kitchen as it is a bit crowded in here.'

There was a kind of holy hush in the kitchen as Mrs Finchcock laid the object on the table and unwrapped the tea towel to reveal - a large plate.

'Would you *Adam and Eve it*?' Joe struggled not to grin.

'Oh Esther!' gasped Kitty.

'I can see why you thought it inappropriate!' was Alex's response.

'This must be what Melissa was looking for!' Izzie declared.

But before there could be any further discussion Xavier, Midge and Sasha ran into the kitchen.

'That's the rude plate I told you about!' Sasha told Xav. 'It is so rude they have to keep it hidden away.'

Chapter 22

George and Betty's Reaction

'I can see why Sasha thought it was a "rude" plate.' George Oxley laughed and took another look. Kitty had rung her parents as soon as everyone had left and they had dropped everything and driven over.

The plate lay on the kitchen table in all its blatant glory.

'You're sure this is what Melissa was looking for?'

'It must be. Alex and Joe checked the scullery, storerooms and washhouse just to make sure but there was nothing else hidden away.'

'We like Alex, don't we George? He seems so unaffected and friendly.'

'He is Mum. It is because of him and Joe that, at last, we … I'm getting Stoney Lea sorted out.' Kitty smiled; it wasn't just having an orderly bedroom that was so great but she really appreciated - no liked - having Alex around.

'Have you found anything?'

Betty Oxley looked up from her tablet. 'There's a lot of information and some images. I'll read some of it out.'

Kitty moved her chair closer to her father's and leaned her head on to his shoulder. George and Betty had been shocked when she'd told them of Tom and Melissa's affair. Like everyone else they'd thought that Tom and Kitty had been the perfect couple. Online detective work about the plate was a welcome distraction.

'So, it says here that English delftware pottery with its painted decoration is similar in many respects to that from Holland. However a peculiar English quality is the more relaxed tone and sprightliness …'

'Our plate is definitely …

Betty glared over her glasses at her husband before continuing. 'Throughout the history of English delftware; the overriding mood is provincial and naïve rather than urbane and sophisticated".'

'So it's English?' asked Kitty.

'I think it must be as it's definitely not sophisticated.'

'There's some quotes from experts and then it goes on to say … oh this is it! "Blue-dash chargers, usually between about 25-35 cm in diameter with abstract, floral, religious, topographical or patriotic motifs, were produced in quantity by London and Bristol potters from the early 17th and into the 18th

century. As the chargers were kept for decoration on walls, dressers and side tables, many have survived and they are well represented in museum collections. Their name comes from the slanting blue dashes round the rim."

'Oh! Listen to this; "One of the most popular decorations on blue-dash chargers was a representation of Adam and Eve with the serpent in the Garden of Eden, produced from the 1630s to the 1730s" – just like this plate.'

'If it is the real thing.'

'Do you think it might be a replica?'

'Don't know . . . we'd have to ask Melissa about that.'

'If you two will just let me get on the next bit is very interesting. "The challenge of rendering the anatomy of Adam and Eve was inescapable, and as the subject became freely repeated by painters of less competence, most of the anatomy gave trouble, particularly Adam's abdominal muscles".'

The three of them peered at Adam's anatomy, which appeared to be accurately and well painted.

Betty peered at the screen. 'It says that, "These eventually became grotesque and could not be wholly covered by his fig-leaf. In later examples, the images had declined to the level of coloured *graffiti*; Adam and Eve were cave dwellers, the Tree had become a mere cipher and only the serpent and the fruit proved simple enough to survive debasement."

'I don't think that that last bit refers to Kitty's plate.' Betty took off her glasses. 'Both Adam and Eve are well painted and so is the tree and the fruit. The serpent …'

'Looks like Melissa,' declared George and gave Kitty a squeeze. The thought of the plate covered with seductive fare, which, as they were consumed, would reveal more and more of the wanton figures was both intriguing and repulsive. Melissa of all people! How could Tom have been so dick-headed to treat his wonderful, beautiful daughter like that?

'Kit-Kat, have you looked if there is anything on the underneath?

'Yes,' Kitty turned the plate over. 'There are some marks: an askew black B and four dots in the shape of a diamond and a wonky H and a kind of bow with an arrow through it.'

'They'll be the potter's marks and should will make dating it easier.'

'There's also a paper label stuck on – it says Beecham & Black Antiques 2014.'

'Beecham – like the pills?'

'Yes Dad.'

108

'Well, don't pull it off as it'll be useful for provenance.' Betty and George were fans of television antique programmes and knew that 'provenance' was everything.

'Kitty, love what are you going to do with it?'

'I don't know, Dad.' Kitty frowned. Her initial reaction had been to smash the monstrous plate on to the kitchen's flagged floor but Mrs Finchcock's presence had stopped her. Somehow she didn't want to appear uncontrollable and hysterical in front of Alex and his mother.

Izzie had asked her if she wanted to challenge Melissa but Kitty felt she needed time to think about the situation before igniting what could turn out to be a major family row.

'I need time to think it through a bit more,' she kissed her dad's head. 'Dad, be a pet and make us all a cup of tea. I'm going to ring Rollo.'

Chapter 23

Rollo's response

'Kitty, I have to be honest with you – I knew Tom and Melissa were having an affair.'

Kitty put down her lasagne-laden fork and stared at Rollo. Her mind as well as her stomach churned. Rollo – the one person in the entire world she trusted, relied on and loved like a brother had known of Tom's infidelity before and during the long, lonely months since his death.

'You never said anything?'

'Would it have helped or made things easier?'

'Yes … no … I don't know.'

Kitty picked up her wine glass and stared into the ruby depths. 'How long had it been going on?'

Since Kitty's phone call Rollo had given considerable deliberation on how he'd answer this question. He too had felt betrayed by Tom's adultery, as like Kitty, he had loved Tom.

And because of that love he'd confronted his friend as soon as he suspected that he was becoming involved with Melissa.

Tom had laughed it off by asserting it was just "a fling … a bit of fun" and that they weren't hurting anyone and especially Kitty or Chris, his brother. He sincerely believed that as long as Kitty didn't know then everything was all right. He loved his wife and his wonderful children and their life at Stoney Lea and he had no intention of letting this affair become serious. And it was a reciprocal arrangement; Melissa had assured him that she felt the same. They'd see each other for sex and a good time and that was all. No strings attached.

But when Rollo expressed his opinion that Melissa was just the tip of a very slippery slope and there'd be others after her Tom had become incensed. Now, Rollo's quandary was that he didn't want to besmirch his friend's memory or hurt his wife anymore than necessary.

'How long had it been going on?' Kitty repeated her question.

'About a year.'

'A year?' Kitty attempted to stand but sank back on to her chair. 'The affair … when did it begin?

'Tom was very disappointed that you didn't share his vision for the Jackson-Johnson.'

'That bloody car!' Tears filled Kitty's eyes. 'It's responsible for everything.'

'He thought it was a fantastic opportunity to make a fortune. And he was right; what has the museum paid for it?'

'A quarter of a million,' whispered Kitty.

'He knew it was a long-term project but in the end ...'

'His children had to live in an unfinished building site.'

'I offered to loan him the money.'

'So did my parents but Tom in his pig-headedness refused as he ...'

'Believed in the car.' Rollo chose his words with care. 'His ... pride was hurt when you didn't share his enthusiasm or see the potential of his ... investment.' Rollo picked up his glass, 'and Melissa was very understanding.'

'So she seduced him.'

'Something like that,' Rollo took a mouthful of lasagne; it felt like cardboard in his mouth. 'Tom told me she really listened to him and became excited about his ideas and plans for the car.'

'She would be – the moneygrubbing two-faced cow.' Kitty wiped away the hot angry tears that were now pouring down her cheeks with her napkin. 'Mark says I shouldn't refer to her as a "cow" as it is unfair to cows.' She stared at her wedding ring and tried to control her anger with her napkin angst and resentment. 'Tom and I quarrelled over it,' she whispered. 'We'd never really rowed before. Even when I didn't want to move to the country we didn't actually argue. Tom won me round, as always, by gentle persuasion.'

Kitty recalled that glorious, golden October weekend nearly three years ago and Tom's wide, triumphant grin as he'd seen her face as they'd driven into Stoney Lea's yard. He would be getting his way and they'd be moving to this rural idyll.

'But this time I wouldn't give in and every minute he spent in the workshop taking him away from me and his ... our family, just fuelled my anger.' Kitty stared across the room, tears still streaming down her face. 'I couldn't help it but my resentment just grew and grew.' Rollo passed her his perfectly folded and ironed handkerchief.

'Even ... that last time,' Kitty continued 'when we went to stay with Sue and Mike he was rushing back to the workshop even while the kids were still waving goodbye and blowing him kisses.'

Rollo passed her his napkin, as his handkerchief was now sodden. 'Do you think Chris knows about it?'

'I don't think so,' Kitty blew her nose on the damask napkin and took a sip of wine.

Rollo considered what he knew of Chris and Melissa's marriage. 'I think he's grown used to turning a blind eye to some of Melissa's activities.' Rollo shuddered when he thought how she had tried to proposition him during the twin's christening party. 'But I don't think he knew about her affair with Tom.'

'Rollo, that last phone call to Tom's phone ... was it from her?'

'Kitty ...'

'Rollo, I need to know.' Kitty knew she was distressing Rollo as he shared her pain but at this point she needed to know.

'Yes,' Rollo's voice came out as a whisper. 'It was from Melissa.'

Kitty felt a wave of relief sweep over her. When she had rung Tom that fatal morning there had been no reply and for months the fact that her call might have caused his death had been festering inside her.

Once more anger against her sister-in-law rose but she took a couple of deep breaths and it subsided. 'It's now too late to stir things up but I'd like to make Melissa suffer as I ... we have.'

She began to clear away their plates of uneaten lasagne and the salad bowl when she stopped and sat down again.

'Rollo, the plate! We can do it through the plate.'

'How?'

'It might be valuable. Mum did some online research and if it is genuine and not a replica it could be worth quite a lot.' Kitty laughed. 'Melissa was always turning up with a plastic box of something that needed decanting into a large dish or bowl. Remember how she demanded one at Tom's funeral for her "special fruit salad"?'

'And upset Mrs Finchcock at the same time.'

'Dear Mrs Finchcock – if only she'd realised that she was the one who knew where the plate was hidden.'

'Come on Kitty,' Rollo took the plates of her. 'Let's think what to do while you make the coffee and I do the washing-up.'

Chapter 24

Provenance

'Hello. Stoney Lea and Sasha Munroe speaking. Who do you wish to talk to?'

'Sasha, its Rollo and you must never give your name or your address over the phone. You never know who might be ringing. Mummy must have talked to you about it.'

'Yes, she has,' there was a pause. 'So, how do I know that you are the real Rollo?'

'Good point but I am Rollo - your godfather and I need to talk to your mother. So, please will you go and tell her.'

Sasha giggled. 'I knew it was you because you've got Rollo's voice. I'll get Mum.'

On the other end of the line Rollo heard Sasha bellow, 'Mum, the Godfather is on the phone!' Even if Kitty is out with the hens, he thought, she'll hear that.

'Hello Rollo,' Kitty sounded breathless. 'I was just collecting the eggs when Sasha called.'

Yes! Rollo grinned to himself. 'Hello Kitty, I've been to see Charlie Beecham.'

'Of Beecham & Black?'

'Yes, I visited their shop in Chelsea yesterday at lunch time …'

'And?' Kitty felt apprehensive and excited at the same time. Discovering the provenance of the plate was essential if she wanted to get back at Melissa without directly exposing her affair with Tom.

'They keep meticulous records and our plate was sold in October 2016 to a Professor Hubert Walter, an American professor on a sabbatical from the University of Massachusetts in Amherst.

'While he was living in London, he visited Beecham & Black's antique shop and informed Mr Beecham, that he wanted to "surround himself with the gen-u-ine Olde Worlde England that his kinfolk would've known" and, our plate was one of his purchases.'

'Is it genuine?'

'Mr Beecham said it dated from about 1670 and he sold it to the Prof for £300.'

'£300! Wow!'

'And that would include his mark up but he said that Professor Walter had got himself a bargain as there is always a demand for English delftware.'

'So Rollo, we know it's valuable but we don't know how Melissa got her claws on it.'

Kitty heard Rollo laughing at the other end of the phone. 'I'm already on to it. Our professor was over here on a two-year research sabbatical. He's now back in the States and I've sent him an email and have asked to speak to him on Skype this evening.'

'Do you think he's our link to Melissa?'

'I hope so or I'll have buy myself a deerstalker and a calabash pipe.'

At the other end of the phone Kitty giggled, 'Well, if it comes to that please let me be your Doctor Watson.'

'Elementary, my dear Kitty, I'll let you know how things stand after the call. Bye.'

Kitty put the phone down hoping that this American Anglophile was the connection they needed.

Chapter 25

Further Provenance

It now seemed quite natural for Alex to stay on for supper. He'd come over that afternoon to check some measurements for the new scullery and to get Kitty's approval for the plans for the old washhouse. Together they decided to keep the old copper as a feature. After all it was Holly and Ivy's favourite retreat.

At present Kitty found her resentment towards Tom and Melissa diminishing. At intervals it still appeared in waves of bitterness for instance on the occasions she'd had to console Sasha or Midge when the realisation that their Daddy had "really-gone-and-was-never-ever-going-to-come-back-ever," came flooding back.

That evening, after an impromptu picnic in the garden Alex organised a rowdy game of French cricket followed by hide and seek which spread into the kitchen garden with Midge and Harry the definite winners and the runner beans the sorry losers.

With Xav, Alice and Harry returned to their respective homes and Sasha and Midge finally asleep Kitty started to prepare a civilised, grown-up meal. She found she enjoying cooking for Alex just as she had for Tom after they'd completed the children's bath and bedtime routine.

She was still thinking about Alex as she made a salad and so neglected to stir the hollandaise sauce. There was something about him that attracted her. It wasn't the immediate 'wow!' she'd felt when she first met - no, saw - Tom across a room. He'd rescued her from the dullest and dreary halitosis sufferer imaginable. Kitty knew she was in love with him even before, later that night; he kissed her just below her right ear.

And now he was gone. She was certain he'd never stopped loving her or the children; the fact was it hadn't been enough to stop him having sex with another woman and that woman, his conniving sister-in-law. But, she was adamant she was not going to blame herself. She knew she was right in thinking that the family should've come first before that bloody car.

It helped to think of them just having 'sex' rather than even considering Tom to be in love with someone who wasn't her as that was just too heartbreaking to contemplate.

As Kitty scraped the curdled sauce into the bin she thought of what Alex had told her about his own marriage and how he and his wife had drifted apart until they were leading separate lives although still living in the same apartment. He'd only found out there was someone else after they'd agreed to divorce and he'd moved out.

Still thinking about Alex she made a makeshift sauce by stirring finely chopped spring onions, dried chilli flakes and chopped capers into some of Izzie's goat's yoghurt.

The village gossips had it that it was something – or rather someone who was bringing him back to Staffordshire nearly every weekend. Such rumours spurred Mrs Finchcock into informing Mrs Shelby and the other worthies who patronised the village shop, that Alex's regular visits to Stoney Lea were because he was overseeing the work in the scullery and renovating the washhouse. The village busybodies, of course, took this intelligence with the liberal pinch of salt it deserved.

Like everyone else, Kitty knew Joe had the work well in hand so there was no need for Alex's frequent visits but they were strangely welcome and the weekends he didn't come to Eden Bridge seemed curiously empty even though there was always plenty going on.

Alex got on very well with Joe and Izzie but, recently, Katie had the feeling something else as he often called in first at the Goat Shed before he dropped in at Stoney Lea.

'The hens are shut up for the night and Daisy seems to be telling Kong a bedtime story,' Alex informed Kitty as he entered the kitchen.

'And what was it about?'

'I didn't like to eavesdrop but I expect it was about a good little donkey and carrots. Is there anything I can do?'

'I'm just about ready if you'd like to put some knives and forks on the table.'

'And glasses?'

'Yes please. There's white in the fridge and a bottle of merlot on the dresser if you'd prefer red.'

'That was wonderful, thank you.' Alex placed his knife and fork neatly together on his empty plate. 'Now, tell me how things are going on with the provenance.'

'Rollo and the professor are getting on like a house on fire.' Kitty laughed as she put down her glass. 'The story so far is that Mrs Hubert Walter – apparently that is how he always refers to her – was not enamoured with his

116

desire to surround himself with remnants of Olde Worlde England; gen-u-ine or otherwise as her predecessors had come from Sweden. She liked the pewter candlesticks and copper jugs but Adam and Eve in the altogether was not to her Lutheran taste.'

'So he sold it to Melissa!'

'Not exactly. Just before the Walter's were moving back to America Melissa went to view their place as she was looking for a flat for a new client. There was the plate and some pieces of Spode on a side table, which Mrs Hubert Walter had also rejected and Melissa offered to take them all off her hands for £50.'

'£50?' Alex topped up Kitty's glass.

'Yes, as it turns out, the professor hadn't told his wife what he'd originally paid for the plate and Mrs ...'

'Hubert Walter ...'

'Accepted Melissa's offer thinking she had made a good deal.'

'The crafty cow – I've never met your sister-in-law but from what I've heard I am not doing her an injustice.'

'You should hear what Izzie calls her! But the beauty of all this is that Mrs Walter insisted on some paperwork for her records and the receipt describes the plate and clearly states, "Sold to Mrs Munroe for £50".'

'Just "Mrs Munroe", no initial?'

'No name and initial and it is signed and dated by Mrs Walter. There's Melissa's squiggle of a signature where the Munroe is more or less legible but nothing else. The professor, once he knew Melissa had diddled his wife, contacted Beecham & Black to check on the current market for English delft, which has risen in value. The original receipt signed and witnessed by his lawyer has been sent to Rollo's iPhone so, for the moment, it will stand up as provenance when I sell it.'

'Are you going to sell it?'

'Yes,' Kitty sipped her wine. 'I thought of donating it to a museum but money is important to Melissa so to get even with her I'm going to sell it.'

Kitty found she didn't want Alex to think she had spiteful nature. 'Alex, I'm not usually a vindictive or a greedy person but between them and the car and the plate, Melissa and Tom ruined our lives and by getting rid of both of them I believe Sasha, Midge and I can truly move on.'

'Melissa might challenge ownership; there is her "squiggle".'

'Rollo had one of his legal friends look into it and we should be all right. We don't think Melissa will want Chris to know. He was very cut up over Tom's death and I don't think Chris would forgive Melissa if he discovered she'd been having an affair with his brother.'

Kitty rose from the table. 'Melissa knows that she has a cushy life with such an easy-going, complacent husband and a comfortable, well-heeled life.' But this time, thought Kitty, she'll find that revenge is a dish best served cold.

Alex followed her into the scullery. As she turned their eyes met and they found themselves kissing.

It was a gentle kiss and not unpleasant although tasting of fish, spring onions and Sancerre. Kitty suddenly felt shy but Alex's smile was so warm and full of genuine affection and without a trace of urgency or expectation, which filled Kitty with a feeling of absolute happiness.

'Early days,' she said to herself she picked up a bowl of plums and greengages.

After Alex had left Kitty went out into the garden. Bats flittered through the air; their cries too high for human ears although Sasha had claimed she could hear them chatting to each other as they flew about. The resident pair of tawny owls called as they swooped across the surrounding fields hunting for mice and voles. The dewy grass felt fresh and cool under her bare feet and as she sat on the garden bench she thought about *that* kiss.

Kitty had been both hurt and indignant when her father-in-law had suggested she found herself "a nice gentleman farmer". At the time she, truly hadn't even thought about another relationship. Since Tom's death she'd survived on a day-to-day basis concentrating on keeping Sasha and Midge loved, contained and secure. But recently there had been so many changes and so many new people in their lives that she had little time to feel lonely. On reflection, there were times when she had found herself missing or even longing for Tom less and less.

Startled by Ivy who was quickly followed by Holly and Arty jumping up on to the bench Kitty gave her life and situation some thought. She was still in her early thirties and, hopefully, there were years ahead of her to consider. She was still young enough to have another child. At present she wanted to stay at Stoney Lea but Sasha and Midge wouldn't be with her forever and would she want to be always on her own.

Alex's kiss had reminded her how she had loved being loved not just in a platonic way but with the passion, consideration and rapport all of which made up a true and loving relationship – something she'd believed she'd had with Tom.

I would like to find love again and be loved, she thought. But will it be with Alex? She was beginning to believe there could be a distinct possibility. But he worked in London and a weekend thing was definitely not on the cards, as it would confuse the children as well as giving the villagers' wagging tongues something concrete to gossip about. After Tom's death there'd been cruel rumours about Rollo's frequent visits until Mrs Finchcock had put a definite stop to them.

Alex was kind, thoughtful and he made her laugh. Not only Sasha and Midge but also all the other children adored him and he had proved to be a good friend and, she decided, a seriously good kisser.

As the moon drifted out from behind a cloud there was an eerie screech as a hungry predator caught a hapless creature. The countryside is a cruel place, thought Kitty. Having someone around on a permanent basis would be nice if only to get rid of the mice and voles that Ivy and Holly and occasionally Arty, brought in as appreciative offerings.

Tipping Ivy off her lap Kitty walked back to the house followed by both cats and the opportunist dog - all of them anticipating an extra snack.

Chapter 26

Rounding up Izzie's story

Rollo carried the glasses into the garden. The evening felt close and heavy as if a thunderstorm was brewing. A solitary blackbird was singing from the top of the lilac tree while overhead house martins swooped through the heavy air. The Friday traffic had been horrendous and now he felt tired and unable to relax. Not only a tricky problem at work would demand his attention over the weekend but his responsibilities to Kitty and the children and now her friends were also in the equation. It was at times like these when he really missed Tom. Just being with him had made Rollo feel lighter, funnier and somehow, more real.

Just like Kitty, we all need time, he thought and, as in confirmation, there was a loud hee-haw from Daisy and Kong's paddock.

'Sorry about that,' said Kitty as she joined him in the garden. 'It was Beth. She'd arranged for an au pair to start at Manor Farm next week and this evening she's had a text to say she's not coming.'

'Where did they find her? Through an agency?'

'They were going to go through an agency but Melissa's current girl recommended her. Beth and Mark liked her and thought she'd be suitable.'

Rollo sat up straight, 'What was she called?'

'Not sure … it was something like Ursa … no, Erszi … Erszi Baranyi. Alice thought it sounded like "barn" and therefore very appropriate for someone coming to live on a farm.'

'Where was she from?'

'Not sure but Melissa's au pair is from Hungary. Do you think it's significant?'

Rollo was obviously thinking through this information. 'I've come up this weekend as I've news for Izzie that I prefer to tell her directly rather than over the phone or by Facebook Messenger.'

'Is it about Tivadar Czinege because this morning Sasha, Alice and I went up to Goat Shed to collect some of Izzie's goat milk yoghurt …'

'Hope you've saved some for me.'

'Of course! Well, Izzie and Xav had gone into town with Joe so I let myself in and helped myself from the fridge as pre-arranged. So, when there was a knock on the door I presumed it would be the postman.'

Rollo put down his glass and lent forward. 'Who was it?'

'A tall, dark hair man who asked if this was *Roses* Cottage and then addressed me as *Miss Blakeney*.'

'And?'

'I denied everything while being perfectly truthful. Goat Shed is *Rose Cottage* and I am not *Miss Blakeney*. I also told him that I didn't know of anyone called *Blakeney*.'

'What was his reaction?'

'He spoke on his phone in an incomprehensible language and then tried to give me a letter addressed to *Izabella Blakeney*.'

'Did you accept it?'

'Of course not as that would imply that I knew *Miss Blakeney*,' Kitty sipped her wine. 'He seemed confused about what to do next so he spoke on the phone again and then drove off.'

'Did you get the number?'

'1HYN 76S.'

'Good girl!' and Rollo, already tapping a number into his phone, left Kitty sitting in the stillness of the deepening twilight.

'Sorry to dash off but I had to report the incident. You should've rung me immediately after it happened.' As he sat on the bench Ivy jumped on to his knee. 'Things have changed; Tivadar Czinege died last night in what are considered suspicious circumstances.'

'Murdered?' Kitty's raised voice caused Ivy to stick her claws into Rollo's knees before leaping off and disappearing under the lavender bushes.

'Maybe; it's not certain, He was found dead in the thermal baths in Zalakros. It might have been a heart attack or – well, he had plenty of enemies and fingers in a lot of dirty dealings - but investigations are in progress.'

'How will this affect Izzie and Xav?' Kitty clutched at Rollo's arm. 'If Xav is the only the heir won't Tivadar Czinege's people come looking for him? Are they still in danger?'

'I'm not sure although the word on the street is that Tivadar Czinege had kept his existence secret but it'd be best if they went away for a while.'

'I'm due to take the children for a week to Sue and Mike's caravan in north Wales. She could go there instead of us or there's Joe's place in the Lake District.'

'I'll talk to her in the morning as I might have some answers by then.' Rollo checked his phone before getting to his feet. 'Kitty, can we go inside: the midges are biting me to death?'

Chapter 27

Serenading Goats

'So, you are happy to keep an eye on the place while we are away?'
Izzie was gazing intently at her son sprawled on a rug eating a ham and tomato roll while discussing the pro and cons of donkeys versus ponies with Sasha and Midge.

Both Izzie and Xavier had taken to dress in a less flamboyant and colourful way. Although Izzie, in navy trousers and the shell pink T-shirt wore them with her usual nonchalant flair and style.

Izzie picked up a piece of discarded cucumber from the plate. 'You know that man called at the Post Office? Mrs Selby rang me as he was asking about *Roses Cottage* and *Miss Blakeney*.'

'No! I hadn't heard. Was it before he went to the Goat Shed? What did she tell him?'

'For a start he'd really pissed her off as his car knocked over two of the tubs of geraniums outside the shop and he didn't apologise. She did tell him how to find Goat Shed but she said there definitely wasn't anyone called *Blakeney* living there or in the village.' Izzie sighed. 'I'm hoping now Tivadar is dead Xav and I will be safe and left in peace.'

Kitty gave her arm a squeeze, 'Rollo will let you know how things are going and don't worry as we'll keep an eye on everything. I've got the number of your new phone and Joe's so we can keep in touch.'

'Thank you for letting us have your holiday. Xav is excited about staying in a caravan. After our week in Wales we're going up to Applethwaite. Joe wants to clear up the house and his workshop and put them on the market.' Izzie paused, 'He's going to move in with Xav and me.' She laughed at Kitty's amazed face. 'Well, he can't sleep in the bothy forever and Xav is OK with it and so am I.'

Kitty gave her a hug. 'I'm really happy for you both but, will there be room? If Joe brings his stuff down from Cumbria where will he put it?' Kitty felt she was on a roller coaster ride; and although she'd just coped with one rapid descent before she was off towards another heady rise. 'And will he be bringing more of his tools with him?'

'Yes, we hope you'll let us store them in the workshop for a few months at least. Will that be all right?'

'Yes, of course although it doesn't seem much of a favour.'

'That's not the favour,' Izzie began to plait the fringe on the end of her favourite silk scarf. 'I wonder if you'd look after and water the veg garden while we were away.'

'Sure, no problem.'

'And the goats.'

'The goats?' Kitty was stunned. 'I know you've showed me how to milk them but I couldn't get the knack of it. Midge was better at it than me.'

'Mark or Geoff will come and milk them but they do like company and if you sing to them ...'

'Sing to the goats?'

'They like civilised conversation as well but singing does wonders to the milk yield. Gilda likes anything by Abba but Drusilla prefers English folk songs.'

'You mean "*nymphs and shepherds come away ... fal-a-la-la-la-la ...*!" sang Kitty looking horrified.

'That'd do – at a pinch,' laughed Izzie. 'It shouldn't curdle the milk.' She looked thoughtful before continuing. 'I'm sorry to get you mixed up in all this.'

'That's what friends are for.' Kitty gave her a hug. 'If you can't help out when a bit of cloak and dagger is needed then you're not true friends.'

'And that is what we are,' Izzie wiped a tear from her eye. 'Rollo is right we should get away until what exactly happened to Tivadar is established.'

'Are you ever going to tell Xav about his father's family?'

'When he's older and it depends on how the investigations about his grandfather's death – official and unofficial – turn out.'

'If you like we'll hang on to Xav while you pack and remember when we do go on holiday you'll be looking after the hens, Ivy, Holly, as well as Daisy and Kong and I'm sure they'll all appreciate serenading.'

'Will do and with a hey-nonny-no!' laughed Izzie.

'That'll be a "neigh-nonny-no" in Kong's case,' replied Kitty.

Chapter 28

A Chance Caller

Midge, dressed and ready since half past six was too excited to eat much breakfast and was now slowly driving his mother and sister demented with his loud eagerness.

Mark was fulfilling his promise to take Midge and Harry on the quad bike with him when he went on the Hatherstone Hills to check his sheep. Kitty just hoped that her little son's high expectations wouldn't turn out to be a let down.

'Don't forget to say "hello" to Dilly and Dally when you see them.'

'They won't remember me,' Midge's voice took on a wistful tone. 'But it would be nice if they did.'

'They most likely will,' Kitty reassured him. 'Beth told me that hand reared lambs are always friendlier towards humans so say "hello" from me too.'

Mid-morning, with Sasha and Alice dancing ahead of her, Kitty walked up the lane to entertain the ruminative nanny goats with her best musical offering. She still wasn't sure if the singing was a necessary factor to the goats' equanimity or if Izzie had been pulling her leg.

Goat Shed looked chocolate-box perfect in the August sunshine. The goats were now digesting their breakfast and, no doubt, pondering on Sasha and Alice's heartfelt rendering of a medley from Disney's *Frozen*.

The cottage garden was full of bees and butterflies and the two little girls, still singing, ran about the tiny lawn as Kitty began to deadhead the roses growing around the front door.

'Excuse me, but is this Rose Cottage?'

Kitty turned and the singing stopped. There was a young woman leaning out of the window of a small blue car.

Sasha and Alice, well primed in "stranger-danger," drew close to Kitty. The woman was fair-haired and had a friendly, open expression but that could just be a clever ruse.

Kitty was still considering her answer when the woman got out of the car and came towards the gate.

'I'm Frances Saxon. The lady in the Post Office said I'd find my father here.'

'You're Frannie?' Kitty felt relieved but before she could say anything else Sasha took charge of the situation.

'Have you got proof that you are who you say you are?'

Alice joined in the interrogation, 'There are nasty strangers about and we have to be sure you aren't one of them before we speak to you.'

'A driving licence or a passport will do,' insisted Sasha.

'Well, I am Frannie Saxon and I have my driving licence with me but my passport is at home. I didn't think I'd need it to enter Staffordshire.'

Alice solemnly looked at the driving licence and the two girls carefully scrutinised it before handing it back.

'Thank you Frannie,' said Sasha opening the garden gate. 'Perhaps you are tired after your journey; may we offer you some refreshments

'We only have goat's milk but it is fresh.'

Kitty tried not to laugh as the two little girls led the way into the cottage. They were so polite and serious with their offer of hospitality. Following them into Izzie's cottage she was curious to find out how Frannie had tracked her father down.

While Kitty made the coffee Sasha and Alice discovered that Frannie was now a staff-nurse at Ligbury Hospital and engaged to a doctor, called James. Once the plate of biscuits had been passed round and the offer of sugar declined they became bored with the restrictive role of hostess and went back into the garden with Xav's Lego box to construct an equestrian centre for a whole herd of multi-coloured Lego ponies.

As they drank their coffee Frannie told Kitty how she'd traced her father. Once again the Jackson-Johnson was the key.

Joe had accompanied the car to its new home at the Brooklands Museum, as Kitty hadn't felt up to going with it after all the trauma and trouble it had caused.

Rollo had met him at the museum and the handover had gone smoothly. The museum director, obviously delighted with their new acquisition had invited the local and the national press to cover the occasion.

It was seeing her father on the local TV news that alerted Frannie to his whereabouts. She had made enquiries at the museum, which resulted in getting Eden Bridge's location and Kitty's address.

'Dad and I used to be so close but after my mother and grandfather were killed in the accident we were so taken up with salvaging what we could from

126

the flood and filling in forms for the insurance that we never really took time to comfort each other or talk about our loss. Neither of us took time to properly grieve. After the burial everything seems so strange and unreal that I tried to submerge myself in my studies. The flood had affected the whole village and made everything seem illusory. I wanted to stay with Dad but he insisted I went back to uni and I … left him on his own.'

As Kitty listened to Frannie she felt her pain.

'I must admit I didn't go home as much as I should've done but it just didn't seem like home. Dad was drinking more than he should and he was neglecting the business and then we were flooded again and I just I couldn't take it anymore.

'My last year at uni was tough and I was struggling emotionally, financially and academically so I decided to stay on over Christmas and work. Then Applethwaite was flooded for the third time. Whenever I tried to ring home Dad was never there and his mobile was switched off. I even called the pub to see if they knew where he was but all I was told was that he'd packed up the van on the 21st December and left the area.'

Tears were now streaming down Frannie's cheeks. Kitty's cheeks also felt moist as she passed Frannie Izzie's box of tissues.

'Your Dad turned up here in early May. Your Dad had been sleeping rough in his van but it was stolen and he'd lost his phone and absolutely everything. My children found him in the lane and installed him in the garden bothy for a couple of days until I … discovered him.' Kitty laughed, 'he's been living in the bothy all summer and now seems part of the family.'

'You and Dad are?'

'No, I don't live here. We've just come to see to the goats and water the veg plot. I live at the farmhouse back down the lane. Your Dad was in the bothy there.'

'But the lady in the Post Office said I'd find him here.'

'Your father is … has started a new relationship with Izzie. He … they are on holiday at the moment but are planning to go up to Applethwaite next week.' Kitty wasn't sure how much she should reveal or say about Joe and Izzie's plans. 'I can ring him if you like.'

'Oh! Please do.'

Leaving Frannie in the cottage Kitty went into the garden. The equestrian centre had been abandoned and now a Lego trail led to the raspberry cage where Sasha and Alice were stuffing themselves with the ripe fruit.

'Joe? No, everything's fine but your daughter, Frannie is here and would love to speak to you.'

Leaving Frannie, simultaneously laughing and crying over the phone, Kitty left her and joined the girls among the raspberry canes.

Chapter 29

Plans for the Workshop

'Hi Kitty. Have you spoken to Alex recently?' Joe entered the kitchen carrying a basket of pears.

'Not since he was up for the Bank Holiday weekend.' Kitty folded the last of the empty shopping bags and turned towards Joe. 'Remind me never to go shopping on a Saturday morning ever, ever again. Coffee and a doughnut?'

'That would be great but I'd like a quick word first.'

Joe held the kitchen door open letting the September sunshine flood the kitchen. He indicated that he'd like her to go into the yard. Kitty thought that he looked a tad nervous.

'I don't want to speak out of turn especially if Alex hasn't mentioned anything but we ... I want to talk to you about the workshop.'

'Joe, if it is about storing your stuff in there don't worry about it. I have no use at all for the wretched place and, as you know, for two pins I'd tear the place down.'

'Its not about my stuff – well, not directly.' Joe unlocked the workshop door. 'Alex and I have been thinking that I could start up a new business.'

'Furniture making?'

'Possibly or maybe making custom-built kitchens and bedroom fittings. I've really enjoyed doing your place up and Mrs Finchcock's attic. I've been asked to make bookshelves for a new library in the Old Rectory over Mayfield way so Izzie and I think there is the real possibility of building up a local bespoke business.'

That will mean they'll be staying here, was Kitty's immediate thought. After Frannie's visit there had been the suggestion that Joe, Izzie and Xav might all move to Cumbria.

Izzie must feel that she and Xav were really safe and that there wasn't a threat of repercussions after Tivadar Czinege's unforeseen and sudden death were her second thoughts.

Rollo had told Kitty that the official account of his death was a massive heart attack and if there'd been anything untoward; it was, officially at a very high level, being well and truly hushed up.

She knew that Rollo had flown to Budapest and spoken to colleagues attached to the embassy and, on his return, had a long and intense talk with Izzie and Joe; resulting in Izzie kissing him with tears running down her cheeks and Joe grinning like an idiot and shaking his hand until Rollo had begged him to stop.

Joe brought Kitty back to the present by pointing to a section of the yard. 'We would have to allocate that part of the yard as a customer car park, if that is OK with you? We'd need to check on planning permission, of course, and we'd pay you rent.'

Kitty nodded. If the workshop could become something useful and positive that was more than fine with her.

'I don't know if I'm speaking out of turn but Alex wondered if you had any plans for the old shippon?'

'The shippon - don't you mean the cowshed? Well, I wasn't thinking of becoming a milkmaid ... *"all forlorn milking the cow with the crumpled horn"*, if that's what he wants to know.'

'Oh Kitty,' Joe grinned. 'I can just see you at five in the morning, on a three-legged stool, milking a docile black and white Holstein.'

'I think a gentle sweet eyed Jersey would be more me. Anyway I was useless at milking the goats so there is no way I'm going to attempt to milk a cow.' Kitty dismissed the vision of herself dressed as a Dresden milkmaid and turned her attention to Joe's original question. 'Why is Alex interested in the shippon?'

'He thinks it might make a good office or a studio. There'd be plenty of natural light from the skylights if they were enlarged and the windows look out on to the field and could easily be made bigger. The outward appearance of the building from the yard or the lane wouldn't be altered. With the outside stairs the old hayloft could become a mezzanine workspace if a decent roof-lantern or observation dome were fitted. What do you think? Daisy and Kong's loose box and the one next to it wouldn't be touched so you'd still have plenty of storage.'

'I don't know.' Kitty felt thrown by Joe's suggestions. 'Beth once suggested that we might start a farm shop and although I hadn't given it a lot of thought seeing as Beth won't be doing much until after the baby is born. We thought the shippon would be ideal and there'd be parking in the yard.'

'Aye, that could work really well though you'd need planning permission and there'd be food and hygiene regulations to be put in place as well as staff training. I know a bit about this as Mandy, my wife's cousin, changed the old

130

village hardware shop into a café and gift shop. She had folk in suits with clipboards crawling all over the place during the refurbishment and for months after she opened as well.' Joe studied the yard's cobbles. 'You'd also need to consider the local competition.'

'You mean the shop at that huge fruit farm near Leek?'

'Aye, and there's that cracking farm shop the Prunehill side of Eden Bridge. They sell that wonderful Sage Derby and those fabulous chilli sausages and they have a café.'

'Well, I don't have to make a decision yet as there's loads of time to think about it. Beth's baby isn't due until the beginning of November. But I'll talk to Alex next time he's here.'

'It's Alex who is hoping he might have it as a studio.'

'What?'

'He's thinking about moving back and starting up his own architectural business. With Danny on board for electrics and plumbing we'd work together on projects as well as working independently.'

'So, you've got it all worked out and, naturally,' Kitty felt herself becoming hot and angry, 'I suppose I'm the last to know what's going to happen to my workshop and my shippon.'

Joe looked guilty. 'We were going to mention it when he was last up but the weekend was so busy what with the cricket match and the village barbeque and the skittles challenge.'

Kitty nodded. Over the Bank Holiday weekend Stoney Lea had been full of visitors ranging from her parents, Rollo and Sue and Mike and their children. On top of all this, Frannie had brought her fiancé, James, to meet Joe, Izzie and Xav.

Alex had been part of all of the gatherings but there hadn't been time to have much more than a few moments of snatched conversation. He hadn't made any further moves to corner her into a romantic situation although he'd been paired with her in the skittles championship. But since the kiss Kitty definitely felt there was something special between them.

'I'd like your permission to start the proceedings for converting the workshop and, if you agree, with Alex's idea, for the shippon. We'd need to put in a loo, washroom and a little kitchen. Clients, as well as us, will need facilities and a brew.'

'I'll need to think about it and speak to Alex. It's a lot to take in.' Kitty frowned. 'Once changes are made anything I might want to do disappears.'

'Such as?'

'Well, the farm shop or ... I could turn the shippon into a holiday cottage.'

Joe gave the idea some thought. 'That would work. Plenty of people like to stay in the country and there are loads to do and see around here. Think about it Kitty; speak to Beth and to Alex.'

Joe paused wondering if he should add one more piece of information. 'Izzie wants to stop faffing around with her arty-farty craft things and to focus her creativity at a more professional level and would like to use the converted hayloft as a studio.'

'Izzie?'

'Yes. She's very talented and she's keen to really use those talents.'

Kitty felt she'd had too much to take in. 'Joe, I need time to think it all through and, as you said, to talk to mum and dad and to Rollo. Oh, excuse me ...'

Kitty retrieved her phone from her pocket. It was Rollo with news about the plate.

Chapter 30

Thoughts

The residents hunting owls were still calling to each as they swooped across the night sky.

They must've caught enough supper by now, thought Kitty, who had counted at least fifteen twit-t-whoos as well as over a dozen screeches and eeks while she waited for Alex.

Alex had phoned the second she'd finished her call from Rollo. Joe must've rung him as soon as Kitty had gone inside to concentrate on Rollo's call.

The plate was now in the hands of a leading London auction house. Rollo's news was that their ceramics expert had recommended increasing the reserve and this helped to dissipate some of the anger and annoyance Kitty had felt over the way her so-called friends had conspired over the shippon. Kitty was now longing to browse their online catalogue to see the plate.

Consequently, she was able to listen to Alex in a calm and reasonable way.

'Kitty, I'm sorry I should've discussed everything with you before now. It started out from a casual idea and … just escalated.'

'And you didn't think to discuss that "casual idea" with me?'

'Kitty, we … I was wrong and I do apologise. Look, I'm working today and am at an onsite meeting at the moment but I'll come up as soon as it's over. Kitty, we've come so far that we mustn't let a misunderstanding come between us.

'OK, OK, I'm coming.' Alex paused. 'Sorry about that but I must go. I'll see you this evening. OK?'

As soon as Alex's had rung off Kitty walked down the lane to where Beth was leaning on the gate and watching Sasha and Alice leading Daisy round the paddock.

'Look at Kong!' laughed Beth. 'He is exactly two paces behind his mum and when she stops, he stops and when she turns, he turns. Well done, Daisy! You have brought your little son up beautifully. I hope my baby will be just as obedient.'

'So, it is a boy?' As Beth and Mark were being very secretive about the sex of their baby Kitty and Izzie were vying with each other to see who could be the first to discover the big secret.

'You'll just have to wait and see.' Laughing, Beth patted her bump. 'Just a few weeks more and then everyone will know.'

The girls were now running alongside Daisy as they urged her from a walk to a gentle amble.

'Beth, do you remember when we talked about opening a farm shop?'

'Kitty, when I'm pregnant fecundity takes over and I sometimes have difficulty remembering my own name.' But Beth paused and thought. She had come up with the idea, in a vague kind of way, during one of their lazy summer afternoons.

'We'd been picking raspberries and there was such an abundance that the idea did occur to me and ... we did talk about selling the excess and ... yes, a farm shop was mentioned.'

'Do you think it was a serious idea?'

'I don't think so. I haven't given it any more thought and then, as I've said, I get really cow-like when I'm pregnant and then my blood pressure rocketed during the hot weather. My doctor thought I had pre-eclampsia.

'I think I was talking about what I would do after the baby was born - restarting tango classes was somewhere on the list.'

Beth now gave the idea some serious attention. 'Kitty, is it something you really want to do? It'd be a lot of work and there would be endless regulations to meet.' Beth's practical farmer's instincts came to the fore. 'You'd have to source stock as well as you couldn't rely on just your own produce.

'There's local competition as well; there's the shop at the pick your own fruit farm near Leek and the farm shop at Prunehill, just the other side of Eden Bridge. Their Sage Derby is as good as my granny used to make and Mark just loves their chilli sausages.'

Kitty nodded: she'd called in on her way home from the supermarket and bought Sasha and Midge's favourite pork and apple bangers for supper. 'I was just wondering if a shop would be possible as Joe and Alex have plans for the old shippon.'

'Yes, Izzie was telling me how she hopes she'll have a studio in the hayloft.'

Kitty felt her resentment returning. 'Everyone seems to know what's going to happen to my yard before I do. Do you all think I need protecting or am unable to make decisions for myself?'

'Kitty, it wasn't like that. Izzie was telling me how they were a bit cramped in Goat Shed since Joe had moved in. She wants to really make something of her skills and a proper work area would give her opportunity to do that and make more room in the cottage.' Beth grabbed Kitty's arm and pointed towards the two girls and the donkeys.

'Oh! Look at Sasha! She's a natural little rider.'

Kitty turned and there was her daughter, riding round the paddock, on Daisy's back.

'My turn!' Alice insisted as Daisy quickened her pace to take the carrot from Beth's outstretched hand.

'Sasha, you shouldn't be riding Daisy. She might've thrown you off.'

'Aw Mum, we've been riding her for weeks and she really likes it.' Sasha climbed on the gate to give her mother a hug. 'When Kong is bigger Midge and Harry can ride him.'

'Not for a year or so until he's grown and is much stronger.' Beth looked thoughtful. 'But, Sasha, you shouldn't ride without wearing a hard hat or a body protector.'

'Alice, nip home and get both for you and for Sasha.'

The two girls ran down the lane towards the farm. Beth stroked Daisy's soft nose and rubbed her ears. 'When I was young my grandfather had Shire horses which he still used on the farm and in ploughing competitions. My brother and I used to gallop bareback on them round their field whenever we could.' She laughed at the memory, 'we were in really big trouble if we were caught but that didn't stop us.

'Mark has picked out a pony for Alice for Christmas and that'll be nice company for Daisy and Kong as they can share the paddock. Will that be all right with you? She lowered her voice, as the girls returned accompanied by Midge, Harry and an enthusiastic Arty. 'But please don't say anything to Sasha.'

Kitty felt a stab of jealousy for Beth and her family circle. That is what she and Tom once had and Tom had thrown it all away like one of the oily rags in his workshop.

As she started preparing supper Kitty made a list of all the reasons why she should or shouldn't turn the shippon into a farm shop.

PROS

1. Own boss

2. Reliable income

135

3. *Working from home*

4. *Using own + local produce*

5. *Café & maybe some crafts (talk to Izzie)*

6. *Develop new skills - computer, financial*

7. *Benefit for the community - more visitors to the area.*

CONS

1. *More responsibility - Lack of independence*

2. *Will need new skills in finance & computing*

3. *Initial outlay + Insurance - buildings, equipment, & stock.*

4. *Major upheaval during refurbishment. The children - may have to work weekends & holidays even with staff*

5. *Sourcing stock/being taken in/ put upon by suppliers*

6. *Alex!*

A really good farm shop could become a local asset, thought Kitty, and something that could be really good for her, the children and the village.

But, while the potatoes boiled and the more she thought about it, the idea became less and less attractive. The children would hate it if she were tied to the shop at weekends and during the school holidays. Even if she employed staff she would still be responsible for the business side of things. On top of this, Beth hadn't been really serious about the scheme.

The self-catering idea wasn't really an option although, as Joe had mentioned, it was feasible. But getting the place spotless on changeover days and having strangers coming and going all the time wasn't something Kitty couldn't seeing herself doing or enjoying.

On reflection, she decided adding butter and milk to the mashed potatoes; the farm shop and self-catering argument had arisen through pique.

Would she have felt different if Joe, Izzie and, especially, Alex had discussed their plans with her from the start?

Alex. How would he explain himself and was there an ulterior motive for wanting to have his new workplace at Stoney Lea? Maybe he thought he'd take advantage of their friendship and get a rock bottom deal on the rent. Or maybe, she thought, as the sizzling spitting sausages brought her back to reality, he just wanted to be near her.

Lamplight glowed through the windows into the yard and the children were in bed and the kitchen tidied of the weekend clutter by the time she heard Alex's car pulling into the yard.

In spite of finding time to shower and her mind and face fully made up Kitty still felt nervous as so much depended on this evening and what Alex had to say.

Holly and Ivy sat on the garden wall and watched Alex drive out of the yard. Kitty stood until the tail lights of his car were out of sight. She felt ecstatically happy and knew she had a ridiculous grin on her face. So, when a cold, wet nose nudged the back of her legs she just swept Arty up into her arms, kissing and nuzzling his head.

Jealous of this canine attention the indignant cats jumped down and clawed at the hem of her dress to get their share of attention. Once inside all three took advantage of her blissful state as she lavished treats on all three of them.

Even if she wanted to Kitty couldn't fault Alex's explanation. She'd already known he'd become increasingly dissatisfied with his job and London life but it was discussing Joe's plans for his new business, which had prompted the idea to move back to Staffordshire and start up on his own.

The area was prosperous and if extensions and barn conversions were not the height of his architectural ambitions they would be a start and provide an income. But on a more significant level Alex knew that it was Kitty he wanted to be with more than anyone else. That was the crux of the matter.

Kitty had burst into joyful tears when he told her he wanted to be part of her life, which included Sasha and Midge and that he loved her.

During the evening Joe's workshop, Alex's office and a studio for Izzie became accepted facts although secondary to their feelings towards each other.

In some strange way Kitty now had a sense of being liberated from much of what had happened to her and to the children; redeemed by Alex's feelings for her and there was now the possibility of a brighter, happier future.

Kitty knew it was different from the way she'd loved Tom. That had been instantaneous and she's been immediately swept up into his hectic life. With Alex, there had first been friendship and attraction, which had developed into love.

Nothing had been said that evening about the future, as both Kitty and Alex knew they must take things slowly because of the children, although Kitty hoped it wouldn't be too slow. But there was the understanding that Alex would be at Stoney Lea a lot of the time and not just for work.

Kitty shooed Arty out of the kitchen and encouraged him to return to his own home. How would the cheeky little dog feel when Alex got his own, much longed for dog?

Taking advantage of Kitty's reflective mood Holly and Ivy sneaked up the kitchen stairs and curled up on her bed. When she came upstairs, after locking up, Kitty hadn't the heart to shoo the crafty cats back downstairs.

Chapter 31

Oliver

There was quite a gathering at Manor Farm to be introduced to Frederick Piers Willoughby. A furry rabbit and a sleep suit covered in blue and green elephants had been presented by the Stoney Lea contingent with coloured pencils and felt tips for Alice and a red racing car for Harry.

Izzie had made him a jazzy patchwork cot blanket in shades of blue and white and there was craft paper and scissors for Alice and a blue racing car for Harry who was aiming for his own F1 team.

Beth, the proud and optimistic mum, had declared she'd be fit and ready to join her friends at their weekly tango sessions by the beginning of January.

After the baby's head had been well and truly wetted with either champagne or elderflower cordial and he'd been passed round to be admired and cuddled it was time to return to Stoney Lea with all five of the children. Kitty needed to remove the three dozen baked potatoes from the Aga and get them and everyone well wrapped-up for the village bonfire and firework celebrations.

But as everyone were putting on coats and scarves the farm dogs set up an almighty racket of frenzied, angry barking.

'It is most likely a fox passing through the yard,' said Mark going towards the door. 'There's a really cheeky one about so I hope your hens are locked up for the night.'

'They are,' Midge told him. 'We didn't want them to be frightened by the noise of the fireworks as it could stop them laying.'

As soon as the door was opened Arty rushed out and followed Billy and Spark up the lane, all three barking furiously. Leaving Beth and baby Freddie in the warmth everyone hurried after the frantic dogs.

A van, with a trailer attached, was parked in the lane. The ramp was down and the gate to Daisy's paddock was wide open. In the field there was someone with a torch and a clanking bucket.

'Shit, bloody rustlers! Everyone quiet.' Mark ordered punching 999 into his mobile. 'Joe, shut the gate.'

'They are after Daisy and Kong?' squealed Sasha.

'Hush, keep quiet,' whispered Izzie, 'until we know what's happening and how many there are.'

'But we must save them.'

'We will,' declared Midge. 'Bad men aren't going to steal our donkeys!'

Kitty put her arms around Sasha who had begun to cry.

The van, which was old and beat up, was empty and unlocked. Joe reached into it and removed the key while Mark spoke to the police.

'We're in luck,' he told them. 'A car is on the way. The police were en route to the Eden Bridge bonfire.'

'There's a pony in the trailer,' Xav commented. 'It's got a blanket on its back.'

The three dogs, which had stopped barking on Mark's command, began to growl as a man, hauling Daisy by her halter, walked across the paddock followed by the obedient Kong.

'Good evening,' said Mark.' May we help you?'

The man and donkeys came to a halt. The man looked at the formidable trio of Mark, Alex and Joe leaning on the gate, the growling dogs and at Kitty and Izzie with the children clustered behind them.

'I've just come for me donkey,' muttered the man. 'Me name is Midgely, Darren Midgely and this 'ere is my donkey.'

'Prove it.'

'Look, she knows me.'

'She knows there are pony nuts in the bucket and that's what she's after,' Alice declared. 'She loves treats.'

'Look, she's mine and I've been looking for her night and day since she went missing.'

'When was that?' asked Kitty.

'Weeks ago.'

'When exactly?'

'It was at the beginning of ... August. That's it ... 3rd August to be exact.

'But Daisy has been here since ...'

'Alice, hush,' ordered Mark.

'Yeah, I've been looking for 'er ever since. Me kiddies will be that pleased to get 'er back.'

'What's her microchip number?' asked Sasha who had now recovered from her tears and was eager to play her part in the interrogation.

'Chip? She ain't chipped.'

'All donkeys and ponies are chipped,' Sasha stated. 'So, she must be chipped.'

'Well, she ain't. Now let me through as I know me rights about me own property and this is my donkey.'

'And that presumption gives you the right to break into a field and take it away?' Mark held the gate firmly shut.

'Well, there was no one in the 'ouse when I knocked so for everyone's convenience, like, I just thought I'd ...'

'Commit trespass on someone's land and help yourself to someone else's property.'

'Nah, she's mine mate'

At this point, Kong, not used to being ignored and aware there were pony nuts in the bucket, gave the man's arm a gentle nudge. Immediately the man cuffed him followed by a stream of obscenities.

As Kong squealed, Daisy, the protective mother, brayed and lunged; biting and kicking until the man and bucket were flung to the ground.

Mark vaulted over the gate and grabbed hold of Daisy's halter pulling her away from further trampling leaving the swearing, squirming rustler lying in the mud.

Along the lane a siren was heard and a car with its flashing blue lights pulled up by the trailer.

By the time the police had made their arrest and taken preliminary statements from everyone it was too late to go to the village bonfire.

From Stoney Lea's yard glittering blue, red and green starry trails could be seen filling the evening sky while faint cries of 'oohs!' and 'ahs!' came over the smoky air whenever a chrysanthemum of light filled the sky with gold and silver jewelled stars.

Daisy and Kong were safely installed in their loose box while the pony, liberated by the police from the trailer, was munching hay in the spare stable. Sasha and Alice were busily plotting how they could keep him and were visibly disappointed when the vet, arrived to verify his chip and locate and notify the owner.

'Do you think that dreadful man might be Daisy's owner?' Kitty wanted to know. 'We still don't know where she came from.'

'I doubt it,' said Mark. 'The police say that the whole of the Midgely clan are well known to them as regular charlatans and conmen. They have "form" as the saying goes. The pony had been nicked as well and Midgely most likely had buyers for both Daisy and the pony already lined up.'

'Alice, will you please stop tugging at my sleeve. The answer is still no. We can't keep the pony. Max is on the phone to his owner right now.' He grinned at his disappointed daughter knowing that when Pebbles, the dapple-grey pony he'd purchased, made her appearance on Christmas Day this poor little pony would be forgotten. 'Now where is Harry? We'd better get back to your mum and the baby. Shame about the bonfire and the fireworks but we'll make it up to you guys very soon.'

'Mark, please take some of the baked potatoes home with you,' Kitty began wrapping up a parcel of the foil wrapped spuds.

Before he could answer Midge came in from the yard and banged on the kitchen table with his fist.

'Everyone, please listen to me.'

So summoned, everyone turned to look at Midge although Sasha took a moment to straighten one of the gingerbread men she'd been arranging in a geometric pattern on a blue and white plate and Xavier pinched a crisp from the bowl.

'I don't want to be called Midge anymore. People might think I am something to do with that donkey stealer and I don't want that. So please start calling me by my proper name – Oliver Thomas Munroe. Thank you.' Midge – no Oliver – gave everyone a little bow before grabbing a handful of crisps.

As everyone applauded Kitty, remembering her busy, buzzy baby experienced a twinge of sadness although at the same time she felt immensely proud of her son.

Chapter 32

Auction House Blues

Kitty, surrounded by scissors, cardboard and woolly bits, checked her phone for the third – or was it the fourth time?

This afternoon the infamous plate was to be auctioned in one of London's top auction houses. Hopefully, someone would fall in love with it and bid a huge amount of money. Better still if two or even three people, yearned to own a seventeenth century English delftware charger depicting a naked Adam and Eve – or, as Sasha continued to refer to it, "a rude plate" then the bidding could go sky high.

At the end of August, with the plate swaddled in acres of bubble wrap and sealed in a box cushioned by polystyrene chips, Kitty travelled to London where Rollo took her to meet Charlie Beecham.

Kitty had been expecting a venerable antiquarian with elbow patches on his corduroy jacket and possibly using a *pince-nez* or half-moon spectacle at the very least.

Instead she was warmly welcomed by a blond, rosy-cheeked, cheerful looking well-dressed man, who looked as if he would be equally at home in a rowing eight or ordering shirts in Jermyn Street.

Over tea, served in delicate nineteenth century Rockingham china, Charlie Beecham confirmed that the plate was indeed the one he had sold to Professor Walter and produced the paperwork to prove it. He also showed them the emails he'd received from the Professor since Melissa had bought it from his wife for £50.

'Ten years ago,' Charlie told Kitty offering her a macron, 'a plate of the same calibre sold at Christies for £30,000. But markets come and go and, at the moment, English delftware isn't fetching anything like that price. However, it never totally goes out of fashion and I reckon that in the right auction your plate could fetch something between six to ten thousand pounds. More if there are several interested parties.'

Ten thousand pounds! Kitty knew Melissa could and had spent more than that refurbishing a guest bedroom but it was still a considerable sum and would really rankle her sister-in-law when the news got out.

'Where do you think we should send it? Christies?'

'You could do that but they have just had a ceramics sale and it might be months before they have another one. I do recommend that you place this plate in a specialist auction as then worldwide collectors and dealers would be aware of it.'

Charlie looked up some details on his phone. Technology had even entered the antiques trade. 'A-ha! Lovefords have a ceramics auction coming up on 28th November. There's plenty of time to get the plate included in their catalogue as well as getting online interest.' He grinned at Kitty and Rollo. 'They are a well-established firm with a big following in the States and in Japan. The Chinese are also dipping their toes in that market. Are you happy to send it to them?'

Kitty agreed and Rollo shook Charlie by the hand and so it was agreed that the plate, which had caused Kitty so much heartache, anger and grief, would be sold at auction.

'Isn't he wonderful?' Rollo whispered as Charlie left them to set in motion the arrangements with Lovefords.

'Yes,' whispered back Kitty. She looked at Rollo. There was a look of pure bliss on his face. She squeezed his hand. 'Careful Rollo,' she whispered back.

'Thanks Kitty but don't worry; I've already had him checked out.'

Having decided not to attend the auction and to get on with her new life Kitty was surprised to find how she relieved she felt that such a painful remnant of the past had finally left Stoney Lea.

Rollo had promised he'd ring her as soon as their lot was called so she could listen to the proceedings. This way she wouldn't make a spectacle of herself by either bursting into tears, whooping out loud or inadvertently bidding for her own property.

Therefore, she was now at home struggling with cut out pieces of cardboard and battling with double-sided sticky tape and staples in the endeavour to make her son a donkey's head mask for the Christmas Eve crib service. Oliver, would she ever get used to calling him that, had demanded that the Team Rector gave him the part as he felt it would strengthen his bond with Daisy and Kong.

All the same, thought Kitty as she struggled with the template, a carrot or an apple would be an easier way to a donkey's heart rather than dressing up as one.

She became so absorbed in her work that when the phone rang it was something of a shock.

'Kitty? Our lot is next!' Rollo sounded excited. 'You should have come as it really is something else – not at all like it is on TV. Charlie says there's been a lot of interest in the plate and he's had a word with one of the officials and they reckon it'll be a hot ticket.'

'Charlie? Is he there with you?'

'Oh yes. He says "hi".'

'Tell him "hello" from me. Rollo …'

'Shush – the bidding has started.'

Even with the loudspeaker switched on Kitty found the proceedings difficult to follow. Apparently the auctioneer had already received a series of bids so the reserve price had already been reached before bidding in the room began. After that it all was so fast and furious that Kitty had to rely on Rollo's excited whispers.

There were two bidders in the room who were interested and two online so between the auctioneer acknowledging online bids and the waving paddles in the room it all became rather confusing. Kitty was aware that the bids were increasing although Rollo's running commentary hindered rather than clarified matters.

Finally, an online bidder and a dealer, who Charlie recognised as a ceramics expert, were left. When the gavel finally went down, there was a round of applause for the final triumphant, bid.

Kitty was nearly deafened by Rollo's jubilant shout.

Fifteen and a half thousand pounds! The plate had gone for £15,500.

Kitty didn't know what to think or say. There'd be a percentage and VAT to pay to the auction house but that would still leave a considerable sum. Kitty sat down on the kitchen Chesterfield, aware that Rollo was still on the phone.

'Kitty, Charlie says it is best if we leave now before he starts bidding for some Meissen which he covets but knows he can't really afford. Lovefords will be in touch in a day or two but we're going off to celebrate – don't worry it won't be at your expense.'

'Thank you Rollo and thank Charlie, for everything. Go and have a wonderful time and I'll speak to you later.'

The excitement and emotion the auction had evoked churned inside Kitty's head and stomach. The plate – or rather *that* plate - had moved on out of her and the children's lives. Although she was relieved, tears begun to pour down her cheeks.

When she finally stopped crying she became aware of the rather sombre stare of the half-finished cardboard donkey's head. Kitty knew she'd have to make it look like a much more joyful Christmas donkey.

Chapter 33

Chris in the kitchen

'Kitty? Kitty, are you there?'

Kitty came out of the scullery to find her brother-in-law in the kitchen.

'Hello Chris, I didn't hear you knock. Are Melissa and the boys with you? Coffee?'

'Yes please. The boys are at five-a-side football. I thought it best to come over on my own.' He sat down at the table and began to fiddle with Sasha's abandoned felt tips and her clutter of glitter and homemade Christmas cards.

'Kitty, what have you done to upset Melissa? She's in a real state. I've never seen her so distraught or so … angry.'

Rollo had warned Kitty to expect Melissa to initiate some sort of confrontation, as the results of the auction would eventually be in the public domain – certainly on social media. Kitty had, therefore, given it some serious thought. But as it was Chris who'd turned up she had to rapidly think how to handle the situation.

Looking at his agitated face and the way he was doodling fish and cartwheels on one of Santa's sacks Kitty was sure Melissa hadn't told him the entire story. Making the coffee gave her a little time to think.

'Mel says you've committed larceny,' muttered Chris, colouring in teeth on a red, glitter pen shark.

'Larceny? I don't think so.'

'She says you sent something belonging to her to an auction and it was a valuable piece.'

'I sent two of the Clarice Cliff jugs to the village auction in aid of the church roof. Did she mean them? They fetched a really good price although there was a little chip on one of them.' Kitty gently pushed the plunger on the cafetière and poured out two mugs of strong coffee. 'The Redmans left them when they moved. They said we could keep anything we found in the house. I checked with Mrs Redman over the Clarice Cliff. ' Kitty passed a mug over to Chris. 'I've kept the big one as it's cracked. We've started using it as a milk jug.'

'It didn't sound as if it was a jug Mel was angry about.'

'What was it? If I've committed a crime I want to know what it is I'm accused of. Do you want milk?'

'No thanks.' Chris took a sip of his coffee. 'She wouldn't say what it was but, Kitty, I've never seen her so angry. She was chucking things about and swearing like a ...'

'Fishwife?' Kitty couldn't resist the cheap gibe.

'Chris, if Melissa wants to accuse me of something she had better come over and do it to my face. I can't admit to something or deny it if I don't know what it is I'm supposed to have done.' Kitty paused before continuing. 'I want you to make it very clear to Melissa that anything I have got rid of, at an auction or elsewhere, is what was found at Stoney Lea.' Kitty took a sip of her coffee. 'As far as I know the only thing that Melissa has lost in *this* house is an earring and, according to Danny, the plumber, she's already made a thorough search for it.'

Chris stared into his mug. The coffee was very strong and he wished he dared ask for some sugar. Deep down he knew there was more to Melissa's anger than the sale of a couple of old art-deco jugs. But did he really want to know what was at the root of it all? Melissa may have sworn like a fishwife but was there anything fishy involved in all this?

Their marriage wasn't perfect but they had the twins and when Melissa was happy they muddled along just fine and, on the whole, he'd prefer to leave it that way.

'Mel and I - we're not like you and Tom were.' He chanced a weak grin. 'I don't think we've ever felt like friends or real partners.' Chris ventured another sip of the cooling coffee. 'I was always a bit jealous of my little brother. He seemed to have the perfect life especially after you bought this place.

'Sorry, Kitty that was tactless of me. I miss Tom, I really do. Oh God, I really do and I know Mel does. Such a great ... loss for us all.'

Kitty moved round the table and put a comforting arm around her brother-in-law's shoulders whose tears were now dripping on to the ring his mug had made on the glittering shark, now wearing a red, felt tipped Santa's hat.

'We all miss Tom but I've got the kids and I'm trying to make a new life for us all. You have your family and we all have to work with what we've got and love them whatever life throws at us.' Kitty felt tears pricking her own eyes but she knew she had to be strong and resolute for the sake of her own family and for Chris and his boys.

'Chris go home and tell Melissa what I've said. Make sure she understands that I have nothing of hers and she has nothing of mine nor has she the right to anything that is or was mine.' Kitty took a deep breath and tried to defuse the situation. 'I know you will get her to calm down although it might cost you a Caribbean holiday and a whole new wardrobe of designer clothes.'

Chris wiped his eyes before he drained the rest of the coffee. He managed to give Kitty a weak smile. 'You know my wife better than I do. At least you didn't say shoes. I'd better be getting back.' He picked up his car keys along with the spoilt Christmas card. 'Will we see you over Christmas?'

'I don't think so. Anyway, I expect you will be on a beach somewhere hot, sipping mojitos.'

Kitty could see that Chris was already on his phone as he crossed the yard. She wondered was he calling Melissa or looking at comparison holiday websites in readiness of defusing his wife's wrath?

I hope that is it, she thought as she carried the mugs into the scullery. At least I've given him a gentle variation of the truth to take back to Melissa. But surely even Melissa had sussed Kitty's revenge.

Although a despondent Chris had been easier to deal with than a spitting, enraged Melissa, Kitty felt the need to speak to Rollo.

Chapter 34

Christmas Eve

The village church looked and smelt wonderful in the soft glow of dozens of ivory coloured wax candles. Swathes of brightly berried holly and dark green ivy decorated the windowsills and had been twined round the pulpit and rood screen while a huge Christmas tree, glorious and twinkling with white fairy lights and festooned with tiny red-robed choir boys and angels, reached up towards the ancient beams.

Kitty, squashed into a pew with Alex, her parents, Rollo and Charlie, had her fingers crossed that her over excited family and its attendants would behave themselves.

The strains of *Little Donkey* filled the church and, as if aware of the magnitude of the occasion, on cue, Daisy stepped daintily along the central aisle led by a worried looking *Joseph* and with *Mary,* clinging on tightly, on her back. The poignant scene was somewhat spoilt by the verger, in his dark blue cassock, solemnly following them, although at a respectful distance, with a bucket and a coal shovel.

Izzie watched the proceeding from the back of the church where she was making sure the kings and pages' headdresses stayed intact and no one had hidden the gold, frankincense or the myrrh before their big entrance. Mrs Selby had informed her that one year an aerosol of lavender furniture polish, hastily wrapped in Christmas paper, was presented to the baby Jesus.

During the last verse *Joseph* the carpenter and his young wife *Mary* precariously clinging to Daisy's saddlecloth arrived at the chancel steps where three belligerent looking innkeepers met them.

As innkeeper 3, allowing the nicer side of his nature to surface, offered his stable to the sacred travellers Daisy's role was now finished. Innkeepers 1 and 2, followed by the ever-vigilant verger, led Daisy back along a side aisle and into the church porch where Kong and Joe were waiting with carrots.

Mary and *Joseph* were installed in the stable, surrounded by a variety of children portraying farmyard animals including Oliver in his magnificent donkey mask and Mrs Selby's grandson dressed in his beloved Spiderman costume. To the simple strains of *Silent Night* the *Angel Gabriel* accompanied by a host of angels of various sizes arrived carefully bearing a duly swaddled Freddie, to be delivered to the waiting *Mary*.

If, as some of the congregation noted, two of the attending angels were a tad over attentive it was because Alice and Sasha regarded it their official duty to watch over the sleeping baby. Beth, sitting in the front pew and ready to dash forward if necessary, could only smile and wipe away a few gently shed tears.

Attention now turned to a side chapel where Harry, clutching the crook his grandfather had fashioned for his father, and several other heavily bearded shepherds were engaged in taking stripy, woolly socks out of a large black pot and pegging them on to a makeshift washing line.

Alex nudged Kitty, 'shepherds actually washing their socks on Christmas Eve is a bit of the Eden Bridge Nativity tradition,' he whispered. 'I was once chief shepherd.'

Kitty suppressed a giggle as Mrs Finchcock, sitting directly behind them, poked her son in the back and severely told him to 'shush!'

A mixture of outraged gasps and stifled sniggers followed the third *king* who presented the casket of myrrh with a deep curtsey instead of the well-rehearsed respectful bow.

The Christmas story wound its way to the anticipated conclusion and as the children and congregation joyfully sang *O Come, All Ye Faithful* and the Sunday school teachers and the team rector sighed with relief and anticipated the much needed mulled wine and mince pies, warm and waiting in the church hall, when there was a shout from the back of the church followed by the clatter of hooves on the terracotta tiles as Kong followed by a braying Daisy and a frantic Joe dashed down the aisle.

As the little donkey – who, it turned out, had been frightened by the roar of a couple of motorbikes speeding through the village – careered toward the final tableau another donkey, his mask flying, pushed his way through the choir of angels.

'Kong! Kong! Come to Ollie!' and Oliver, catching hold of Kong's trailing leading rein, safely halted the frightened colt.

Alice and Sasha spread their protective winged-arms around *Baby Jesus* and *Mary* just as Beth rushed forward towards her still sleeping son.

It was all over in a moment. To a round of applause Oliver, now Ollie, led Kong towards the back of the church followed by Daisy and Joe.

The verger was in a quandary. He hadn't known whether to stand by the door, ready to present the brass plate for the retiring collection or to grab the bucket and shovel from behind a curtained cubbyhole and follow the donkeys.

151

Never had the promise of a glass or two of mulled wine seemed quite so attractive. Especially as he knew that the rector had requested Daisy and Kong's presence at the Palm Sunday service.

Chapter 35

Redeemed

The frosty, full moon turned the countryside into a mysterious patchwork of white, black and silvery shadows as Kitty and Alex walked Daisy and Kong along the frosted lane back to Stoney Lea accompanied by an excited assortment of children with coats and anoraks draped over their various shepherds, angels and kings costumes plus a dishevelled donkey with his now battered head tucked under his arm.

As they walked conversation swung between Daisy and Kong's participation in making the Nativity play such a huge success, the thoughtlessness of motorbike riders and the extraordinary number of mince pies Harry and Ollie had managed to consume.

The children's chatter made Kitty smile. She felt so happy and contented. Her parents with Izzie, Joe, Rollo and Charlie would be waiting in Stoney Lea's warm and cosy kitchen with hot chocolate and spicy Christmas biscuits and slices of fruity stollen and in the safety of the spare loose box, Pebbles, Alice's Christmas pony was bedded down ready to be delivered to Manor Farm on Christmas morning.

And Alex was here beside her; laughing at the children's nonsense, making sure Kong's rug stayed in place and a lot of the time with his hand in hers.

So much had happened since the last Christmas, thought Kitty as they walked along; there'd been Joe's, Daisy's and subsequently Kong's arrival and that dreadful drama and possible danger for Izzie and Xav over the Tivadar Czinege business and, of course, Alex.

On such a beautiful night Kitty wouldn't let her thoughts linger on the trouble-making Jackson-Johnson or the discovery of Tom and Melissa's affair or the delftware plate and its significance. That hurt was lessening and, now, all that was left was a faint feeling of disappointment that Tom had deliberately chosen to diminish the love he'd had for her, his children and all that had been precious and special between them.

The New Year would bring a new start as the work on Joe's workshop and Alex's studio was due to start in January and Mrs Drummond, the headteacher had asked her if she'd consider becoming a teaching assistant.

As they approached Stoney Lea Kitty became aware of a change in the children's conversation.

'Daisy will be able to be in the 'tivity play next year as they'll need a donkey,' Sasha declared. 'But Freddie won't be the baby Jesus as he'll be too big.'

'He was so sweet and so good,' that was Alice, the loyal sister.

'So, who'll be the next baby Jesus?' Harry wanted to know.

'It'll be Mum and Alex's baby.'

'Sasha!' Kitty didn't know where to laugh or be cross with her outspoken daughter.

'Well, we've seen you and Alex kissing and you hold hands a lot so you could have a baby,' Ollie informed her.

Kitty tried to snatch her hand away from Alex's but, laughing, he held on to it.

'There's more to it than that,' stated Alice, the farmer's daughter.

'Maybe it'll be Mum and Joe's baby,' said Xav. 'They kiss and hold hands and they share a bed.'

'That's what I mean,' said Alice. 'You have to share a bed to get a baby.'

'Look we're home! You all go into the kitchen while Alex and I put Daisy and Kong to bed ... I mean in their stable and enough of this baby talk. Grandma will have hot chocolate for you all.'

'Mum and Alex should share a bed then we would have a baby Jesus for next Christmas,' Ollie decided patting Kong goodnight.

'But we'd keep the baby forever - not just for Christmas,' declared Sasha.

'What do you think Kitty?' Alex asked as they bedded the donkeys down for the night before checking on the Christmas pony.

'About what?'

'A baby ... bed ... you know.' He wrapped his arms around her and nuzzled her hair as she tried to hold out a carrot towards Daisy. 'I truly love you and I know that you love me too.'

Kitty watched Daisy holding back so Kong could take the proffered carrot. The donkey's maternal instinct was very strong.

She looked up and smiled at Alex, 'I think that it could ... no, would be a very good idea as, yes, I do love you and not just because it is Christmas.'

And, on that Christmas Eve, while Daisy and Kong crunched up their carrots in their stable, Alex gently kissed Kitty before asking her to marry him.

As Kitty accepted with tears of joy, on cue, a shooting star blazed a bright, brief silver trail through the starry night sky and across the frosty fields the pair of tawny owls called to each other.

Acknowledgements

I would like to thank George Boughton and all at GBP Publishing and my agent Mary Rensten and the Society of Women Writers & Journalist and the members past and present of Walton Wordsmiths for their on-going support.

The ceramic department at Christies Auction House were extremely helpful with the initial information about English delftware as were Brooklands Museum.

Thanks too to Nora Hartley for her advice about the kitchen gardens, Kay Lundy for her guidance on tango dancing and to Nick Gott for, once again, providing the artwork for a fantastic cover.

Thank you too to my wonderful family and friends for encouraging me and for giving me time and space to write.

Patricia Jones

2019

About the Author

Patricia Jones was raised in Cheshire and north Wales. During her childhood and teen years she spent many happy times on friends' farms on the Staffordshire – Derbyshire border. With a little 'tweaking' the area became the setting for *Redemption in Eden*.

For many years Patricia was a primary school teacher and came to writing through devising sketches for an amateur dramatic group swiftly followed by joining a local writing group.

Redemption in Eden is her second novel. *Threads of Life* was published by SCRIPTORA (2018). She has also written plays.

She is a member of the Society of Women Writers & Journalists and the Society of Authors and presents the monthly Surrey Bookcase, a programme about books and writers on Brooklands Radio.

She lives in Surrey and is married with four grown up children, three grandchildren and a spoilt cat and writes listening to Mozart, Ella Fitzgerald and Elvis.

www.patriciajoneswriter.co.uk

Quotes from reviews of *Threads of Life*

'Threads of life – a modern day Cranford!'

A Littleton

'The style and descriptive writing draws you into village life and the characters and their relationships.'

Charlotte Tabor

'Hugely enjoyable'

T Lewis

'Patricia Jones has captured the flow of village life and the foibles of her characters.'

B Warburton